OUT

of

BOUNDS

DAWN RYDER

sourcebooks
casablanca

Published by Sourcebooks Casablanca, an imprint of Sourcebooks, Inc.
P.O. Box 4410, Naperville, Illinois 60567-4410
(630) 961-3900
Fax: (630) 961-2168
www.sourcebooks.com

Ryder, Dawn.
 Out of bounds / Dawn Ryder.
     pages cm
  (trade paper : alk. paper) 1. Young women–Fiction. 2. Chief executive officers–Fiction. 3. Alaska–Fiction. I. Title.
 PS3623.I6255O98 2014
 813'.6–dc23
                              2013045385

          Printed and bound in the United States of America.
               VP 10 9 8 7 6 5 4 3 2 1

Chapter 1

CALIFORNIA, THE FIRST WARM weather of the season, and a frozen daiquiri at her fingertips... now that was perfection. Monday wouldn't darken her horizon for a full twenty-four more hours.

But Sabra Donovan ended up setting the daiquiri aside. Beyond the sliding glass doors of her beach-front hotel suite, her boyfriend sat on the white sand just above where the waves were washing up. When Sabra had pulled into the parking lot, she was sure Kevin was waiting for her. But a glance at him while he didn't know she was watching told a much different story.

Kevin had his arm draped across the shoulders of another woman. Patty was a friend, one of the group, but the way Kevin's fingers were playing with her nape told about feelings that went deeper.

Maybe she was making too much of it. Sabra picked up the daiquiri, but it just didn't taste right. Her weekend plans crumbled, and she growled when she spied the receipt for the hotel suite.

"Jerk."

The least he could have done was tell her before she blew a sizable chunk of her entertainment budget on a weekend getaway that he really wanted to spend with another woman. Her little tapestry duffel bag earned another muffled insult from her lips.

Definitely no tightly laced corset for him.

She sat down, crossing her legs as she glared at the view of the waves that was costing her three hundred dollars a night.

Stupid idiot.

Crap. She was headed for single life again.

If that labeled her picky, fine. Break out the black ink pen and slap it across her forehead. She was not going to waste any more time with a guy who wasn't as interested in their relationship as she was.

It was a hard truth to face, but honesty was better than ignoring the facts.

Her phone buzzed. It was pathetic just how happy the distraction made her, but beggars couldn't be choosers. Swiping her finger across the screen to unlock it, she stared at the six missed calls from her office. She was an analyst, for Christ's sake; there was nothing urgent about her job.

But there was no way she was going to ignore it, because Nektosha Industries was one of the most elite companies she'd sent her résumé to. She was still giddy to have landed the position. Even if they had an iron-clad rule about everyone starting in a cubicle.

Sure, it was humbling for someone with a master's degree, but she'd wanted the job because she just couldn't help but covet one of the mysterious positions on the sixteenth floor. If the only way up was through a cubicle, she'd park her butt in one for a while.

She wasn't afraid of proving her worth.

A company phone had come with the job, adding a glimmer of hope that her function wasn't completely that of peon. The fact that the little piece of technology was chirping for attention on a weekend offered her a real slice of hope that her time in the bland, beige-colored partitioned walls was drawing to a close. No one needed an analyst on Saturday afternoon.

"Hello?"

"Sabra?" her office manager asked frantically. "Thank God you answered! Look, this is going to sound crazy, but you need to get dressed to impress right now."

"What for?" Sabra asked. "I'm not even home."

"I know where you are," Deanna informed her in her

all-too-familiar, knowing tone. The woman managed the third floor of Nektosha with an iron hand. As far as office managers went, she was a piranha. "All the company phones have location chips in them."

"Silly me."

Deanna clicked her tongue, the subtle reprimand mixing with the sound of the surf. "I'm going to ignore that tone because I'm desperate. There was a blizzard in Alaska and most of the development team is stranded. The reception for the launch of Nektosha's new line is tonight."

"Crap." Nektosha produced a line of all-terrain vehicles. They were rough, tough, and savage. The main testing and development center was in Alaska for that very reason. Launch nights were major events. "Don't you want a VP for this?"

Deanna made a noise that sounded a lot like muffled profanity. "Yes, but it seems none of them are answering their phones."

Deanna's tone made it clear there was going to be hell to pay on Monday. Sabra didn't need to hear it though; even in her cubicle she'd been expected to be fully versed in the new product line. Every employee was. The product line was Nektosha, and anyone who wasn't fully on board with the company wouldn't be working there. As a team member, she was expected to be able to answer any question, at any time.

Team member sounded a whole lot better than *bean counter*.

"I need you to get dressed and over to the Garden Towers to represent us. Mr. Nektosha is not pleased with the lack of company personnel and you are close enough to the event to make an appearance."

"I've got limited options as far as wardrobe goes," Sabra explained, "just the suit I wore to the office."

"It's a suit." Deanna ended the call in her brisk, abrupt way. Chitchat wasn't her style. In fact, most of the senior staff at Nektosha operated in the same go-for-the-throat manner. Meetings on the sixteenth floor of the posh tower she worked in called for large amounts of soothing wine afterward.

Or so she'd heard.

There was no way she was doing time in a cubicle if there wasn't something really great in the works. Nektosha offered her the position title of team member and that kept her confidence high that she'd be moving up. So what if she was working on a Saturday night? It sure beat reporting to work every day with a company that let you know you were insignificant and very replaceable.

Nektosha just felt different.

Her phone chimed with a text, kicking her into action. She tossed her swimsuit on the bed and hurried into the bathroom. The owner of the company would be there, as well as numerous big dog investors. Someone might be unemployed by Monday for ignoring their phone.

It wasn't going to be her.

She took a quick shower and toweled off as the idea of being on Deanna's good side settled into her brain. It was worth walking away from the sunset. But she cussed when she realized her nylons had been tossed in the trash on Friday night in a vain attempt to be reckless and fancy free—at least for as long as the weekend lasted. She looked into the plastic bin but it had been emptied by the cleaning staff.

She didn't have time to buy another pair, which only left the thigh-high, lace-edged stockings she'd packed to complement her corset. Heat teased her cheeks as she opened her bag and pulled them out. She threaded each one carefully up her leg because there wasn't time for a run to ruin one. Pulling out the garter belt that went with them, she hesitated for a moment before securing it around her hips.

No one would know she had it on.

That was a disappointment in itself. Satin garter belts were made to be appreciated. Hers wouldn't be tonight.

Her suit looked drab after she put it on, though—its only saving grace was that it didn't button to her neck. The sapphire blue wool was good quality and the fit was nice, but there would be men there wearing Armani. The color worked well with her dark hair. She ran a brush through it, but there wasn't time to wash it, and even if there was, her hair had a mind of its own when it was freshly cleaned. She gathered it up and started to reach for a hairpin but her reflection stopped her.

Christ. She looked like a spinster. A virgin one too.

It was a party, not a courtroom. Her hair fluttered back down to rest on her shoulders. She pulled her bangs back with a couple of barrettes and gave it a spritz from the hairspray bottle. The sun had left her nose a little pink but a light dusting of makeup covered it.

At least her shoes were new. She slipped into them and gave her hair a last fluff before heading toward the door. Her tapestry bag caught her eye. On impulse, she picked it up.

Sometimes, she thought, fate kicked you in the tail when you needed it. Kevin was someone from her past that she'd been clinging to. Trying to make a relationship work was a mistake, the sort of thing you did before you grew up and faced the world as an adult. Kevin was a kid—a great, fun-to-be-around person, but ultimately a kid. She wanted something else, something more.

The only way to get it was to go looking.

—⁓—

"Do that again and Sheila will be over here to fix your hair again."

Tarak Nektosha glared at his head of security but Bryan Kim only grinned at him.

Tarak tightened his fingers into a fist to quell the urge to run them through his hair. The penthouse suite offered him a stunning view of the San Diego harbor.

He turned away from it.

From the balcony on the west side of the suite, he was able to look down to the garden rooftop where his reception was being set up. The staff was lighting candles on the bistro-style high-boy tables. They already had their vests on and the edges of the tablecloths were sharp from pressing.

Everything was in position, from the banners to the presentation table that held models of his new lineup. Hidden beneath a dark length of silk were the newest creations from his team.

The one stuck in Anchorage.

He ran his fingers through his hair.

His personal staff wasn't enough, not for a launch reception. Below him there were over a hundred men with net worths over ten million just waiting for a chance to buy a new toy. He'd built Nektosha on the quality and rugged ability of its product, but there was still one golden rule that had to be obeyed.

You had to have your hook in the water when the fish were hungry.

"Deanna from accounting is reporting one response."

His secretary's voice came through the intercom.

"Her file is loaded for you."

Tarak tapped in his pass code and the large, flat-screen computer set up on the workstation flickered and brightened. The personnel file was neat and businesslike.

"Master's in alternate fuel," he muttered. "That's a plus."

He let his attention linger on her picture, committing the details of her face to memory.

"You couldn't find someone prettier to look at while you're waiting on me?"

Tarak turned to face Anastasia, but he didn't jump. Anastasia pouted at him and propped one hand on her hip.

"I hope you're planning to appear in something other than that robe."

Anastasia rolled her eyes. She'd already applied a heavy dose of makeup to her perfect features. Her hair was styled to perfection, the blond locks arranged skillfully around her face.

"Don't be pissed off because I caught you looking at other women."

Tarak killed the display with a swift motion of his fingers. "She's an employee. I told you, launch nights are all business."

Anastasia rewarded him with a flash of ultra-white teeth. She wiggled her way across the space between them and pressed a kiss against his lips.

"In that case, I forgive you."

She smirked before making her way back to the bathroom. Normally he would have enjoyed the sight of her nearly nude body, but not on launch night. He turned back to the computer and opened the file again.

Sabra Donovan's picture appeared once again, demanding more of his attention than it should have. She wasn't any sort of beauty, but she seemed to grasp the idea of teamwork that he demanded of his employees. An analyst could be forgiven for ignoring her work phone on a Saturday afternoon, but she hadn't. That was what he was looking for and thought he had in his VPs. He didn't care for the disappointment filling him.

He killed the display and ran his fingers through his hair again.

Her job performance was what mattered. Nektosha was his creation—every model waiting to be unveiled one of his personal works of art. There was one thing he never did and that was get too personal with the business side of the company. The moment it looked as if he were playing favorites with one team member would be the exact moment his office stopped working because it looked like sex was a key factor in advancement.

Anastasia didn't grasp just how important launch receptions were.

At least she hadn't noticed that his cock hadn't stirred.

He didn't need a tantrum to soothe.

In fact, the very fact that he knew Anastasia might throw a fit made him regret allowing her to help him unveil the new line.

His personal life shouldn't be involved with Nektosha business. It was a hard rule that served him well.

It would be the last launch reception he invited a date to. Sabra Donovan was exactly what he needed—a team player who wasn't too distracting. An analyst with a curiosity for biofuels.

Neat, professional, and bland.

~~~

Both feet had to be together when you bowed.

Sabra searched her brain for any more Japanese social customs. If she was going to represent the West Coast office, she had to make a good impression. She was only assuming the owner was Japanese. There were few pictures of him because so many of their products were linked to defense department contracts. Security was tight at Nektosha. So tight, there was a separate set of elevators for the top floors of the building. You could be standing next to a Nektosha VP on the sidewalk and never know it.

Excitement was prickling along her nerves as she contemplated adding names and faces to company titles.

The Garden Towers were impressive even before she made it inside the huge glass doors. Marble floors and an indoor atrium greeted her before a doorman made eye contact with her. She wasn't getting anywhere near the elevators without his say-so.

"Nektosha."

"Your invitation, please," he requested smoothly. It was the perfect greeting; no hint of aggression, his tone as tepid as a summer lake but an obstacle if she didn't have what he wanted.

"Um…" She fumbled around in her purse for a moment before finding her badge. "I'm an employee."

It sounded lame and the doorman's eyes narrowed as he took

her badge. He tapped something into his touchscreen monitor while she fought the urge to squirm. Maybe she should have put her hair up.

"Ms. Donovan, you are on the guest list." He sounded surprised but covered it by handing her badge back to her. "This way, please." He walked toward an elevator tower. He pressed his thumb against a security pad and the door opened.

"Have a nice evening."

The doors swished shut. Sabra looked for the floor buttons, but it was an express car that only went to the top floor. She turned around and watched the street below getting farther away as the car lifted her toward the roof. Faint music filled the car, some piano rendition of the Beach Boys that did little to calm her racing heart. There had never been a better opportunity to make a great impression. The owner of Nektosha never ventured into the analyst department. She was pretty sure he never set foot on any of the lower floors of his own tower—make that West Coast tower. He had more than one. Unlike a lot of megacorporations, Nektosha was owned completely and solely by its creator. Tarak Nektosha had been busy carving out a position for his company among the global elite and he was doing it without a board of trustees.

According to the scuttlebutt, he liked people who thought outside the box and that was a major part of her choice in working for Nektosha. There was opportunity in the company that the old guard would never extend to a gal like her. When you weren't someone's niece, most of the big dogs didn't have advancement opportunities unless you were willing to trade sexual currency for it.

Sabra wanted advancement, but she wanted it because she was good enough at her desk, not on it.

Crude, but still true. Anyone who tried to dismiss the part office liaisons played in promotions was blowing smoke.

The next couple of hours might just define her career, but it felt a lot like opening a volume of Shakespeare. You had fifty–fifty odds of landing in a tragedy.

The doors swished open, revealing a semi-lit entryway. The sound of running water filled her ears as she walked past an indoor fountain complete with koi.

"Welcome. May I take your bag?" A small Asian girl glided up from her post near a small coat closet. Her black suit blended in with the lower light level. She offered a small slip of paper in exchange. Sabra handed her purse over, trying to mask her awkwardness. Being waited on took more practice than most people were willing to admit. She slipped the ticket into her pocket before squaring her shoulders and doing her best to look as though she was perfectly at ease in the high-priced reception.

A large double doorway led the way to the roof gardens the towers were named for. The air was balmy and not too hot now that the sun had set. The sound of the surf mixed with the melody of a string quartet playing discreetly in the corner. The gardens were a mass of greenery and blossoms. The scent of fresh plants mixed with the sea breeze and the flicker of candles lighting the tables.

Posh. Very posh.

A waiter offered her a tray full of drinks. She selected one because it was something to do. Men looked up when she passed, giving her a quick sweep from head to toe before dismissing her.

Her suit didn't scream money and this was a wolf-pack event.

She lifted her glass to her lips and took a sip. The wine was sweet and she peered closer at it. She should have realized the smaller wine glass wasn't to control the amount of alcohol being consumed.

Ice wine.

Of course. It was expensive and unique, like everything else at the event. Off to one side was a buffet table. Even the food being offered was beautiful—little petit fours and amazing looking appetizers. A chef stood behind it, overseeing the staff.

Maybe her garter belt wasn't so out of place.

She smiled and took another sip of her wine. Ice wine was out of her budget, at least for another few years, so she was going to enjoy it.

At the far end of the rooftop, several tables sat with colorful silk scarves draped over them. There was even a velvet ribbon tied across in front of them, just waiting for a cutting ceremony. A photographer with a press badge dangling across his chest from a lanyard was working the lens to get a good shot of the waiting tables. Flashes popped from various other locations around the rooftop as the press gathered their shots of the important people assembled. Some of them had red carnations pinned to their lapels to warn the press they didn't want their pictures taken. Off in the shadows, security men in dark suits watched to ensure the press behaved.

"You are being a bully."

Sabra froze, looking over the rim of her glass. The woman speaking was a sex kitten, from her teased hair to the six-inch heels on her feet. Gold and diamonds sparkled around her throat, and her obviously surgically enhanced cleavage was on prominent display.

"I look wonderful," she insisted.

"You look like an escort. A high-priced one, but a paid companion nonetheless."

The voice was dark.

Sabra lowered her glass, glaring at the contents. Maybe she didn't have the tolerance for ice wine. No one had a "dark" voice. Unless you were five years old and listening to a bedtime story.

Or reading a gothic romance novel.

"The press is here. I can't have you on my arm in that scrap of a skirt. It's a good thing you wax."

Yeah, his voice was dark and razor-sharp. A shiver worked its way down her back in response. It was immediate and uncontrollable.

Yeah, and misplaced. The guy is being crass.

Even if he had an excellent point about how short the skirt in question was.

"This is high fashion. I spent a fortune," she whined, her lips pushing into a pout.

"Of my money, so you aren't out anything but time." His tone was icy and ruthless. The candlelight flickered over devil-dark hair that was longer than most office tycoon's. It brushed his collar and reminded her of a Japanese anime character. It was just long enough to be sexy without looking unkempt. He suddenly moved, turning to catch her in his sights.

She should have turned away or looked away or done something other than lock gazes with him, but time froze—and along with it her wits. His eyes were midnight black and his face chiseled out of stone. In another time, he would have worn a headband and long braids, but the Armani suit did nothing to make him appear civilized.

He wasn't tame, and there was something in his gaze that told her he liked it that way.

The shiver that rippled across her skin said she liked it too.

Her lips went dry and she curled them in to moisten them. Something flickered in his eyes before he took a step toward her.

"You'll do it with me." The sentence was uttered to her with pure intent. But the sex kitten grabbed his arm.

"*I* am doing it with you," she hissed.

Sabra shook her head, trying to dislodge the arousal dulling her wits. It was intense and red-hot, threatening to make a fool out of her because she couldn't seem to recall anything else. The man peeled his companion's fingers off his arm, granting Sabra a second to collect her wits.

Shit! She could feel the insides of her thighs getting moist. The tiny set of panties that went with the garter belt did nothing to mask the scent of her arousal.

"Good night, Anastasia. I don't want you seen like that."

He brushed past Anastasia, and her face turned red and she looked as though she was going to lunge at him, but an Asian man in a dark suit slid smoothly into her path. There was a muffled word of profanity before Sabra looked up at the man bearing down on her.

He swept her from head to toe twice. Heat teased her cheeks and flowed right down to her clit. She was sure she'd never been given the once-over so thoroughly before. At least she'd never felt as if someone's gaze had stripped her. It unleashed a sense of vulnerability that refused any attempts to dislodge it. The fact that she was a modern woman meant nothing in the face of the pure sexual magnetism he displayed.

All she really wanted him to notice was that she was a woman.

"You'll do nicely," he announced, one pace in front of her.

He plucked the wineglass from her distracted fingers and handed it off.

"Excuse me?" she managed to thrust past her frozen lips.

"Sabra Donovan, analyst, master's in biofuels. Correct?"

It sounded as if he only added the last word as a courtesy. There was certainly nothing questioning in his sharp gaze. He knew exactly what he wanted and intended to get it. The pure abundance of confidence was mesmerizing.

"I think you have me at a disadvantage," she muttered.

Pleasure flashed in his eyes. His lips twitched up just a tiny fraction, almost too faint to measure, but she saw it. In fact, she was sure he wanted her to notice. He wasn't the sort who apologized for anything.

Arrogant too.

He was—and completely unashamed of it.

"I'm your boss."

She stepped back, something inside of her recoiling. The hot curl of excitement was lingering in her clit, so she wasn't really sure what it was she objected to, only that complete submission was out of the question. It wasn't a conscious thought, but something she felt on a very personal level.

His eyes narrowed, somehow becoming more sensuous, more determined.

"Excuse me," he offered softly. "Tarak Nektosha, your employer."

She was a complete idiot. He wasn't Japanese; he was Apache. Lawless, savage, and exactly like the line of vehicles his company produced.

"I require someone to help me cut the ribbon," he clarified.

"Oh…" She glanced back at the waiting table. The press was positioned near it, their hands on their cameras; more than one was casting an impatient look toward Tarak. "Sure."

As far as a professional response went, it lacked a lot. But saying "yes, sir" just seemed too submissive. A large part of her flatly rebelled. It was a system-wide rejection, one she was sure she hadn't experienced before in her life. No man had ever unleashed such a bundle of emotions inside her.

Or so much heat.

Get a grip, girl…

And fast too. It was her frickin' boss.

He caught her hand. The contact was jarring. She flinched, pulling free. His lips curled, just a tiny amount, flashing his teeth at her before he reached out and renewed his grasp on her hand. His gaze settled on her lips for a moment, causing her breath to catch.

"They are ready for you, Mr. Nektosha," one of the dark-suited bodyguards informed him quietly.

"Of course."

He stepped forward, settling her hand on his arm. His shoulder rose above her own as he swept her toward the table. She felt petite and scoffed at her own foolishness.

She was wearing a garter belt for Christ's sake.

But you're trembling like a virgin.

"Smile at them…" he leaned down and whispered. "And at me."

He kept a firm hand on top of hers as he guided her toward the tables. The distance seemed to triple as the camera lenses were pointed at her. The flashes popped, blinding her to everything but her escort. Everyone beyond them was just a shape in the shadows.

Tarak was right at home. He strode down the path, nodding at those waiting to see his performance. The quartet played a fanfare as they arrived at the velvet ribbon. He eased her into place, the position of his hand perfect. He just seemed to know how to touch her. One hand cupping her hip and slipping across her lower back to gently push her in front of him. Once he was behind her, she shivered as his size dwarfed her. He caught her hip once more, his fingers spreading out over her belly and securing her in place. The breeze coming off the ocean was cool, but she could feel his body heat against her back. She was still caught in the hold of arousal. Her clit was throbbing and whining for attention.

Her timing couldn't have been worse.

"Thank you. I'd like to introduce one of Nektosha's most valuable assets, Ms. Sabra Donovan, who has kindly agreed to make these pictures so much more appealing by being in them." His tone was full of authority and edged with control.

It was too damned sexy for the setting. Her nipples contracted, leaving her grateful for the practical cut of her suit that hid them. A bright smile was plastered to her face as the flashes popped. Laughter surrounded them as a girl stood nearby with a silver platter. She lifted it up so Tarak could pick up the golden scissors resting on it. He held them out to her and she took them with another little shiver. She'd never responded to a man in such a way.

It had to be the situation.

Which meant she needed to get a grip. Quick.

She concentrated on gripping the scissors and getting them into position. Tarak settled a hand on the small of her back, sending her heart racing again. She closed the scissors quickly and the ribbon snapped. Relief flowed through her but left something bitter behind.

Like regret. Or disappointment.

The waiters grasped the silk scarves and unveiled the collection. Nestled on the tabletop were models of the new line of vehicles. The press surged forward to get shots as the guests applauded.

Tarak brushed her back again. This time it was a longer stroke and slower, as if he were savoring the contact.

Holy shit! The man knew how to touch a woman.

"Well done," he whispered against her ear. The tone was steady and controlled. Too controlled really, because it made her tremble again. He pressed his hand against her back before gently moving it in a small circle. "Interesting reaction, Sabra. One I'd like to explore later."

She turned to look at him, but he cupped her hip and turned her back to face the crowd. "We're still on stage." His hold was strong and insistent, sending a crazy spike of need through her. It tingled and burned a path straight into her pussy, that single grip of his promising her a man who knew how to please a woman. It was savage but too damn hot to ignore completely. There was an undeniable feeling of vulnerability moving through her as she sensed just how little control she'd have in his embrace. He leaned close, brushing up against her body for a long moment. It was electrifying. She had to fight the urge to lift her bottom and brush up against his cock. It was a battle not to, because she wanted to know what it felt like. He leaned down and took a deep breath next to her ear. The skin on her neck beaded with goose bumps and begged for a kiss.

"You smell delicious, Sabra." He squeezed her hip tighter, enough to send a bolt of sexual hunger through her pelvis. "I wouldn't have figured you for the garter belt type, but I approve."

But with the pictures finished, the questions began. Tarak moved in front of the table to discuss the finer points of his new creations.

The press was merciless, but he cut through their questions with razor-sharp confidence. The man radiated sureness.

And it was sexy as hell.

But it was lust. Red hot, but lust all the same. Acting on it, without any other attraction, would knock her down several notches on the respectability ladder. It would also shred her self-discipline.

Like she had any chance of snaring Tarak Nektosha's attention, even for one night of crazy sexcapades. She had to ignore the little comment he'd made in her ear. A man like him was used to flirting outrageously. His net worth alone would have had the women lining up even if he were fat and had a small cock.

She studied him, taking a moment to inspect him. He had broad shoulders that tapered down to a trim waist. There was no hint of spare tire and his hips were lean. His business slacks were slightly baggy, but when he moved, the soft wool gave her a tantalizing view of his trim ass. The front of his pants had several pleats and she decided that was a damn good thing.

She did not need to know what sort of package he had.

Really didn't need to know…

She backed out of the limelight, feeling oddly like a coward, but remaining so close to Tarak smacked of clinging to his coattails too much. There was only one reason a man like him kept a woman in the spotlight with him. Anastasia was a prime example of it too. She was an honest-to-goodness sex kitten, and Tarak certainly looked as if he enjoyed stroking her when he was in the mood to play with one of his pets.

He had a touch that could make a woman purr all right.

The party was in full swing. Those who couldn't shoulder their way into the circle around Tarak moved toward her. Her brain flipped on, rescuing her from the rush of arousal. Numbers and delivery dates were blissfully free of stimulus. Confidence in her knowledge of the company product was its own form of intoxication. There was a thrill that went along with being able to keep up and prove she had merits beyond looking good for the cameras.

Several hours later, she had a small pile of business cards from some of the richest men in the world. It was tempting to indulge herself in another glass of wine, but she decided to be content with her feeling of achievement. Her personal career calendar was a few years ahead thanks to Mother Nature. Okay, maybe she was still heading to her cubicle on Monday morning, but the stack of business cards would make sure she had something more to do than routine number crunching.

"Have some more wine, Ms. Donovan. You've earned it."

The rooftop gardens had a nasty little trick up their sleeve; the lush vegetation allowed Tarak to appear from behind a fern without any warning.

The arousal she'd thought she'd banished flared up, proving she had no control over it. She could feel heat teasing her cheeks, making her forever grateful for the flickering candlelight. He offered her a glass of ice wine, one dark eyebrow rising when she looked at his hand as if it were a snake.

"Oh, yes. Thank you."

She meant to take the glass quickly, but he didn't release it immediately. For a moment, their fingers touched. He relinquished the glass, but not before stroking the back of her hand.

Her nipples tightened. She was pretty sure she'd never been so turned on in her entire life. It was an unquestionable fact that she'd never considered jumping a guy so soon after meeting him.

Not that there was going to be any jumping her boss.

"Thank you for being here, Sabra. Success is highest when we take advantage of passion for our product while it's fresh."

"I couldn't agree more." It was the professional thing to say. But the words felt awkward because her mind wanted to apply a different meaning.

"Do you? I admit I'm curious to see what other topics we agree on. You respond to me so naturally, it's almost possible to believe you are doing so unintentionally. I'd like to explore that topic." His dark gaze slid down her torso to where her nipples were still beaded. A tiny, satisfied gleam flickered in his eyes before he looked back at her face. "Give me an hour to wrap up."

Her jaw dropped. Tarak didn't see it because he was already striding off to speak to an Asian man flanked by two incredibly competent-looking bodyguards.

Like hell they'd see…

Mixing career and lust was a one-way trip to the pavement—or to becoming someone like Anastasia. Besides, the guy's arrogance was off the scale.

She set the wine down and felt as if she'd achieved some sort of victory in doing so. The thing was, Tarak Nektosha didn't need to liquor her up to intoxicate her. Her own raging hormones were doing that all on their own. It would be simple to be pissed at the presumptuous nature of her boss, but part of her was glad she'd had the encounter. Kevin was one hundred percent in her past. She found the little claim ticket in her pocket and went to retrieve her purse. Unlocking the screen on her cell phone, she intended to call him but found a text message instead.

Sabra

I was going to be pissed off about you leaving, but honestly, you saved me from having to tell you it wasn't going to work out between us. Yeah, I'm a chickenshit for not telling you face to face, but I've been seeing Patty for about a month. I'm a dog. Sorry.

She dropped the phone back in her purse and headed for the elevator. There might not be ice wine at home, but there was privacy. Maybe she'd sort out her feelings or maybe she'd just dig out her vibrator.

She reached for the elevator call button but someone slid his hand over it. One of the dark-suited musclemen who had been trailing Tarak offered her a bland expression.

"Mr. Nektosha would like you to remain."

He looked as though it was no surprise to be chasing females for his boss—or taking one away for that matter. Tarak Nektosha owned a billion-dollar company. Those around him jumped when he walked past. Hell, they jumped just to see if they were noticed, and she was no different. As far as business went. Her career was on the upswing and there was no way she was going to cheapen that success by letting anyone get the idea that she'd slept her way into it.

"I can allow you into the penthouse suite to wait for him. He is having some ice wine sent up for you."

The muscleman was pointing her toward a separate set of elevators.

"No, thank you."

She wasn't interested in jumping on command. The bodyguard turned back to look at her. The expectation on his face rubbed her temper.

"But I'm sure Anastasia will be more receptive to that sort of invitation."

Sabra punched the call button on the express elevator before she calmed down. Her temper kept her moving when the heat pooling in her pussy wanted her to stay and make a major fool out of herself.

She wouldn't have to face her vibrator at work on Monday morning.

⁓

The little bottle of ice wine was sitting in a polished silver bucket when Tarak made it back to the penthouse. The cork was still in place and the set of glasses remained untouched.

He should be relieved that Sabra had rejected his invitation. Impulses like that had no place in his business affairs.

That wasn't what was coursing through his veins.

He tugged on his tie, pulling the Italian silk away from his neck. It fluttered down to lie on the sofa as he opened the collar of his shirt and popped open his cuff links. His polished shoes ended up on the small area rug beneath the glass-topped table with the wine. He leaned on the edge of the sofa as he tugged his socks off and tossed them aside.

Better.

The wooden floor was cool beneath his feet and a short walk across the suite allowed him out onto the balcony. This time he faced the beach, tipping his head back to let the breeze wash over the sides of his face. He smelled the surf, but it wasn't enough to banish the scent that had seen him breaking his rule about dating employees.

She'd smelled hot.

And anything but bland.

It had been tantalizing—it still was. His cock was stirring, hardening as he recalled brushing his hand over the strap of her garter belt.

Shit.

She was an employee.

He pulled his shirt completely off, growling slowly as his skin tingled.

He wanted to be naked and he wanted Sabra Donavan naked beneath him.

It wasn't logical, didn't fit into his self-imposed rules, but it was the truth. He turned and headed toward a shower. There wasn't a trace of Anastasia left in the suite, not even a sprinkle of makeup on the marble vanity.

Good.

It was better when his world was operating within the boundaries of his rules. Sabra Donovan would return to those boundaries too.

Even if his hard cock confirmed he thought she was anything but bland.

———

Sunday morning wasn't kind.

Sabra couldn't even blame her sour mood on the ice wine. She'd had less than a glass and that fact only made her more pissy. She'd kicked at the bedding most of the night and her bed was a mess. Sexual frustration was a bitch, or at least it was turning her into one.

Her vibrator had been less than satisfying. A battery-powered toy was no substitute for the reality of the way Tarak had touched her.

Damn! She sounded desperate…

She charged into her chores while her temper was blazing. At least the bathroom benefited from her outrage.

Still, it bothered her to realize just how torn she was. Had she walked out on a golden opportunity to be wild and carefree? Had she turned her back on a golden opportunity?

With my boss?

Yeah, that was always a bad place to go. But still, part of her wondered if she'd passed up her chance to take a sex demon by the balls and ride the lightning.

Ha! He'd have saddled me and made me prance like a pony for his amusement.

There was a really high chance of that being true, but it was also slightly enticing. His voice had just been so damned tempting. Even his arrogance had allure. Part of her just wanted to find out if he was as good as he thought he was.

I'll have to have the guts to grab it, though.

She nibbled on her lip as she finished up her chores. Guts were one thing, but selling out on her ideals was another. Tarak was her boss. She'd gotten her job through her ability and wasn't going to keep it because she screwed on command. Her career plan was in full swing and going smoothly. She was just going to have to find someone else to light her fire.

———~~———

"Mr. Nektosha was pleased with your performance," Deanna announced Monday afternoon.

Sabra fought the urge to cringe and give her office manager any clue to what else Tarak Nektosha had seemed to enjoy. "Thank you."

"You will also be collecting commission on the sales you handled."

"Really?" Now Sabra was beaming and didn't care who witnessed it. Every penny she had was tied up in her new townhome. Being able to feed her starving savings account so soon after closing escrow was going to be a dream come true and a relief, because she wouldn't have to live on Top Ramen.

"Yes," her division boss confirmed. "I believe Mr. Nektosha is making a point to the senior staff about ignoring calls and still expecting bonuses."

She'd agree with that. When money was involved, people tended to get the point a whole lot faster. But she kept her mouth shut because there was no reason to dance on their graves. Behavior like that would be remembered, likely at the most inopportune time for her. Not a single VP up on the sixteenth floor was there because they were nice guys. They knew how to defend their turf.

Deanna peered at her over the rim of her glasses. She was hugging her laptop, which meant she'd come straight down from the Monday staff meeting. Something was on her mind. Sabra could feel her trying to decide what to ask. Deanna imposed a strict, no-personal-information code on the entire department, but it looked as though she was the one debating whether or not to break the rules today.

She blew out a long breath and pushed her glasses up. "There's a recap meeting about the launch at three. Top floor."

"Ummm..."

"You are expected to attend."

Deanna trotted off to her desk, but not before she shot the two accountants on the other side of the cubicle wall a hard look. Their chairs groaned as they leaned back over their keyboards. Sabra looked at the time and her mouth went dry. Fifteen minutes wasn't long enough to prepare.

For what?

The man was a business tycoon. He had his attention on the money, not on whoever had garnered some mild interest during a party. She stood up and went to check her lipstick. A man like Tarak didn't sleep alone unless he wanted to. Anastasia might have been mad, but that wouldn't have stopped the gold digger from jumping if she were called for.

Sabra went to collect her laptop. It was her first meeting on the top floor and she was going to make a good showing. Yep. Her career was on track.

But the elevator ride up felt too long. Her heart was racing and she drew in a few deep breaths to slow it down. She refused to be nervous. This was in her career plan, so it was a moment to be savored.

The door swished open and she moved forward. A large desk blocked the entrance to the dark frosted-glass entryway. A formidable-looking woman sat there. She could have been the mother of the bodyguard who had offered to let her into the penthouse suite. There was a familiar set to her lips and she looked as if she wouldn't hesitate to physically protect her post if it became necessary.

"Sabra Donovan."

"Yes, you are expected. First boardroom on the left." She pressed a button and a faint buzz sounded at the glass doors.

Sabra opened the frosted door and passed through into the cyber brain of Nektosha. There was classified stuff here. Just to get a position on the lower floor, she'd had to submit to a background check. It had been so intense, she was pretty sure they knew about the library book she'd never returned in third grade.

There wasn't a cubicle in sight. Every office had floor-to-ceiling, dark frosted-glass walls. A few faint, muffled sounds made it to the hallway but nothing understandable. Small, glass-domed security cameras were mounted to the ceiling above every doorway.

She turned left and made it to the first open door. The board-room was furnished with a huge table and a dozen padded chairs.

A petite woman sat behind a small desk set off to the side. "You'll want to walk around the table and acquaint yourself with the names of the VPs who will be attending."

Sabra swallowed the lump lodging in her throat. She was heading for a corner office, so there was no reason to panic. Her cubicle was just the bottom step of her career path. Every VP started the same way.

She walked around the table, reading the names and department titles. She circled all the way around twice before sitting down in front of her nameplate. It was very satisfying, even if her nameplate was missing a department title. It was still an engraved one, proving Nektosha didn't penny pinch when it came to appearances.

It was a small thing, but she was marking it as an achievement along the road to gaining what she wanted.

"Good afternoon, Mr. Nektosha."

Sabra was back on her feet. It was another one of those instant reactions, one Tarak didn't miss. His gaze was straight on her as she pushed the chair back. His lips parted again. There was a flash of something in his eyes that set her heart accelerating again.

He was unfairly attractive. Mother Nature was a fucking bitch to make a man so mouthwatering.

At least one that was off limits.

The longer-than-normal business length of his midnight-black hair was still shockingly sexy, highlighting the primal beauty of a face set off with high and sharply defined cheekbones.

None of the normal words like *handsome* or *drop-dead* seemed to fit him. Instead, she was stuck on feelings like *intense* and *untamed*. The perfectly knotted tie and pressed shirt didn't seem to hide it enough. Instead, the civilized business attire looked a lot like camouflage, and she had to fight the urge to back up.

Or move forward and rip it off.

Boss... Boss... Boss...

"Glad to see you could join us, Ms. Donovan."

"Wouldn't miss it, sir."

There. She'd sounded sharp and on top of things. She looked straight back at him and watched him slowly curl his lips. He wasn't grinning, at least not in a pleasant sort of way. In fact, she got the idea he did nothing that wasn't cutthroat. Not in business and not in bed.

Sex demon for sure.

Too bad he was her boss.

There was a scuff on the floor as one of the VPs arrived. Two others hurried through the door, checking their watches as they found their seats.

Obviously Mr. Nektosha wasn't early very often.

Of course not; he was a man others waited on. Any relationship with him would be strictly done on his whim.

A shiver rippled along her skin in response. Logically, she tried to remind herself that he was likely just toying with her. A man like him didn't have to chase women. Inviting her to a board meeting wasn't chasing either; he was making a point to his senior staff—a facet of his character she'd be wise to commit to memory. When it came to business, he expected excellence from his staff. Anything less would result in a lesson.

She was going to muck up her opportunity to impress him if she didn't get her mind out of the gutter.

Tarak didn't sit down. He punched a few buttons on his laptop and the wall behind him flickered to life. The new models he'd unveiled the night before showed up in bold color.

"We launched last night."

The meeting was off at a frantic pace. It was stressful but exhilarating at the same time. Sabra leaned forward and kept her hands on her keyboard as she tapped in notes to look at later. Tarak ran it in a sharp, dry way that could have been called cutthroat. Instead she found it challenging. She wanted to keep up with his pace, wanted to anticipate where he was going with some of his ideas. The lack of title on her nameplate dissipated from her thoughts as she joined in the meeting.

Her action drew several disapproving looks, but she kept her attention on what Tarak was presenting. She hadn't expected a welcome mat. Not here. Among the elite of Nektosha, you had to prove your worth first.

Tarak didn't like the chair waiting at the head of the table. It remained empty ninety percent of the time as he put his hands on the images he was discussing.

The guy was an adrenaline junkie. Hands on, all the way.

She just wished that piece of knowledge didn't make her shiver. Her attention strayed to his hands, the same ones that had stroked her hip so perfectly.

Confidently.

"For those of you who continue to glance at Ms. Donovan while you think I'm not able to see you behind me, in some attempt to remind her of her place, let me enlighten you." Tarak turned around in a sharp motion, making a few of his VPs snap their attention back to him. "She's here because not a single one of you picked up calls from this office Saturday night in spite of the fact that you took other, personal calls."

Tarak rested his fingertips against the tabletop. "There are times we must be ready to adjust, and I expect my VPs not to play games which can cost this company the sort of deals that happen at launch parties. Teamwork is the foundation of this company."

"We were told the design team would handle the launch—"

"The team was coming down from Alaska. Snowstorms have been known to interfere with air travel in that region," Tarak shot back smoothly. "Hiding from the frantic calls of your assistants is unacceptable at your pay grade. The people beneath your feet make a quarter of what you do."

A quarter? Sabra tried not to let her jealousy surface, but her eyes narrowed. Damned fat cats, they could choke on their cutting looks.

Tarak punched something on the laptop and neat columns of cell phone records appeared on the wall behind him. Names were highlighted as well as calls taken during the time of the launch party. A strained silence stretched out.

"If you don't like me knowing your personal call history, I suggest you all purchase a personal cell phone with your own money. As long as this company pays the bill, we have the right to see the call records."

No one moved, but a few faces turned red. She watched it with a strange, detached feeling. Sure, he was being a dick, but at the same time, she discovered herself cheering him on. The fat cats at the top should have to toe the line the same as the rest of the worker bees stuffed into cubicles beneath their posh sixteenth floor offices.

"Ms. Donovan will be joining these meetings for the rest of the quarter, and if she impresses me, as she did this weekend by stepping up when the company needed dedication, she will stay on this floor."

It was as if he pounded a gavel. No one spoke; she was pretty sure no one moved. She didn't even breathe. Tarak took only a moment to make sure his word was law before he left the room.

Every head turned and she was suddenly the sole point of attention. The VP next to her finally broke the silence as he offered her his hand.

"Welcome to the team."

Chapter 2

SHE COLLAPSED BACK AGAINST the wall of the elevator the moment the doors closed. Tipping her head back, she blew out a long sigh. She felt drained, completely wrung out. It didn't seem possible to run such a wide range of emotions in so short a time.

Part of the team…

Well, didn't that sound pretty?

Yeah, pretty scary if she was going to be honest. But she was planning to enjoy every moment. It was that odd little sensation of enjoyment you got from having your insides twisted with just enough fear to make you giddy when you realized you'd survived. She'd just shaken the hands of people who wanted to knife her in the back for doing what they should have. No one liked the boss to have an A student in the house when they hadn't finished their homework.

She was going to make it.

Sure, there were a tough three months ahead of her, but she was going to stuff every penny of her unexpected commission and promotion into her savings account. And she would make it— against the odds, in spite of her single-parent upbringing. She could still see the disdain on the loan officer's face as he'd looked down his weasel-thin nose at her and grumbled about her father's lack of credit, because she really needed a cosigner for her house.

No, she didn't.

In fact, she was about to be able to put her unexpected

commissions into her savings account to give herself some breathing room.

But a quarter?

She'd targeted Nektosha because it was a good company, but she hadn't realized the people at the top made that kind of cash. It was surreal; she really couldn't grasp it. No wonder the VPs had attitude to spare. They were used to a different world than she was.

But there were still some things that were universal. Pleasing the boss man was one.

She smiled on the way to her cubicle but slowed down when she noticed the looks coming over the dull beige partitions—calculating, envious stares, followed by hesitant smiles when she made eye contact. Whispers rose behind her, but she didn't turn around because the two people in her cubicle commanded her full attention. They were packing up her desk. A rolling cart was parked in the aisle with neat file boxes loaded onto it. Deanna stood nearby, overseeing the entire operation.

Her insides twisted and her mouth went dry. Deanna caught sight of her and pushed her glasses up.

"I hope you'll remember all of us down here."

"Why wouldn't I?" The words were stuck in her throat as the last box went onto the cart. The guy who'd loaded it nodded to her.

"We'll get this all settled for you, Ms. Donovan." He calmly grasped the stainless steel handle of the cart and began pushing it down the hallway. People rubbernecked out of their cubicles as it passed.

Her own cubicle was clean, the beige walls bare and sterile as if she'd never been there. Only her purse remained, sitting on the desk top as if it didn't belong.

"I'll transfer all your data. The computers upstairs are operating with more security protocols."

Deanna held out her hands for the laptop Sabra was hugging. Handing it over took more effort than it should have.

"Here's your new badge. Congratulations."

Applause filled the area, proving there were plenty of people listening. The badge card Deanna offered was a sixteenth floor security tag. Her hand shook as she handled it and stared at her own picture.

"All right. Ten seconds of celebration, now back to work. You don't start until tomorrow. Better enjoy the hour of free time today. I hear they work long hours up there."

She believed it. Tarak looked like the demanding sort.

Deanna offered her a curious look before she took the laptop to her office. Sabra reached for her purse and turned her back on her cubicle.

Win or lose, she was taking a big step up the ladder.

Tonight, there was going to be ice wine and she wasn't going to think about how much further she had to fall if she got kicked in the face.

—⁓—

His office was his command center.

Tarak entered it on a smooth, quick stride that didn't draw any notice. His secretary was accustomed to him. Large, flat-screen monitors lined two walls but the other two were rows of windows that could be opened. The damned things had cost a bloody fortune, both in construction and additional insurance, but he didn't care. He needed fresh air.

But that wasn't the craving that was keeping him from settling down with one of the projects waiting for his attention.

It was the way Sabra had looked at him. Her eyes had narrowed and her lips rolled in.

And his cock was rock hard.

There were a dozen women he could call to ease that urge, but he didn't reach for his phone. He leaned over his desk, trying to focus his attention on the monitor.

God damn it!

He grabbed his phone and keys and strode toward the door. His secretary looked up in confusion.

"I'm gone for the day."

She didn't get a chance to respond because Tarak was already stepping into an elevator. He punched the private garage level button and the doors slid shut.

He was out of his fucking mind.

—⁓—

Just because she didn't know what, exactly, her new position was, didn't mean there wasn't going to be ice wine. Sabra wasn't going to let a little thing like a lack of information keep her from savoring the moment.

Whatever moment it really was. Sixteenth floor was good enough.

She took the stairs down to the parking garage, too hyper to stand still inside an elevator. Excitement was making her giddy, and she pulled her new work badge from her pocket as she pushed open the door to the parking level to look at it one more time, just to make sure she hadn't dreamed the whole thing.

Yup, it wasn't a dream. Sixteenth floor. The doors of the elevator opened as she reread the tag.

"I'm glad to see you're pleased."

Sabra stumbled and the badge went flying.

Tarak bent over and retrieved it before she could stop blinking at him like some sort of teenager newly sprung from a girls' school.

The satisfaction on his face pissed her off though.

Arrogant and presumptuous—yeah, he was used to having sex kitten pets, all right. Not that she could really park all the blame at his doorstep. The guy really did emit some kind of primal musk and no one had a body like his without hitting the gym a lot.

He was still holding her badge and one dark eyebrow rose when she hesitated to take it back. He'd lost his suit jacket and tie. The collar of his shirt was open, giving her a look at his collarbone.

Her mouth went dry. She snagged the badge to distract herself, but heat prickled along her cheekbones.

Blushing... seriously?

"Why didn't you join me in the penthouse?" he asked directly.

The badge in her hand suddenly irritated her. "Why did you give me this?"

He crossed his arms and leaned back against the door of a sleek convertible. The thing was midnight blue, which was why she hadn't noticed it. He'd parked right in front of the elevator doors as if he owned the place.

Well, he did.

"Because you put the company first and didn't fold under the pressure of your first board meeting. Do I look like the sort of boss who shares office space with fools?"

She shook her head. "Not really."

"Nice to see I didn't make a mistake. Stuff it in your bag and let's get out of here before everyone leaves for the day. Launch meetings are enough public interaction for me."

She was already doing what he commanded before she realized what he'd told her to do, because he certainly hadn't asked. She wasn't that naïve, leaving with him had only one purpose. "Excuse me?"

He opened the passenger side of the convertible in explanation. "I'd like to take you for a ride."

Oh hell...

Her thoughts went right to the seediest possible ideas.

"Unless I'm just coming on too strong for you."

She clicked her car remote and it beeped behind her. "There's strong and then there's presumptuous."

"There's also dishonest, Sabra."

He moved too fast—or maybe she was just too fascinated with

him. One moment he was holding open the passenger-side door like a civilized man, and the next, he'd slid his hand along the side of her neck and threaded his fingers into her hair.

"You were looking at my mouth as if you wanted a taste."

He cupped her hip and brought her up against his body. He was just as damn hard as she'd dreamed about. Her knees went weak and she was paralyzed by the scent of his skin.

He even smelled sexy. An ache began between her thighs that was so acute she gasped.

"I wasn't."

He brought his head close enough to let his breath tease her lips. She quivered, every inch of her body becoming needy. Her jaw opened, the yearning inside her just too much to ignore.

Tarak took instant advantage, pressing a hard kiss against her lips. There was nothing sweet about it. He fused his mouth with hers as if it were an assault, and she trembled as her will collapsed. Maybe it was because she'd thought about him so much, but she just couldn't keep her hands off him. The temptation was too much and he was too damn close.

She reached for him, sliding her hands over the tight expanse of his chest. But what she really craved was his bare skin.

He left her lips behind as he trailed a row of kisses across her cheek and onto her neck. It was better than she'd imagined it would be, the contact between his mouth and her neck. She shivered as her nipples contracted, and her pussy begged for attention. He stroked her back, his hand smoothing over one side of her bottom before he very deliberately pressed her hips forward.

His cock was rock hard.

She gasped and one of the buttons on his shirt went flying as she clenched handfuls of his shirt.

"Damn it, I want to feel your claws against my skin."

His grip tightened on her butt before he released her altogether.

Her heart was pounding at a frantic pace and she honestly feared she'd stumble without his support. He yanked open the passenger side of the convertible again.

"Get in. We can't get naked here."

There was the flash of pure intention in his eyes. The more she looked at it, the more it resembled victory. Her pussy thought it was a great idea, but her pride balked.

She shook her head and backed up.

His lips thinned.

"You're my boss." She forced the words past her cravings.

"So we can't fuck? Normally I'd agree with you, but I can't seem to listen to my own logic," he cut through her protest ruthlessly. "You want me to swear I won't kick you to the curb with a black mark on your résumé if you get in the car?"

The arrogant tone of his voice really pissed her off. "Like there is anyone to hold you to that sort of a promise."

He drew in a deep breath, looking as if he was actually fighting an internal battle. "I never date employees."

"Glad to hear it." But she wasn't. Nope. She was frustrated and pissed.

"If I didn't have integrity, Sabra, I'd have fucked Anastasia and pretended it was you."

"So you're a stand-up fellow for waiting until tonight. What's that got to do with integrity?"

He glanced at his watch and pushed the car door closed. The first sounds of footsteps came from the stairways. He stepped close again, reaching out to stroke her cheek.

"It has to do with honesty, Sabra. It was your musk that hardened my cock, not hers. That garter belt made sure I could smell just how wet I made you."

He backed up and went around the back of his car. He was in the driver's seat and had the engine on before she recovered from hearing him talk about her body so boldly.

"And if I had no integrity, I'd stay right here for the rest of the office staff to see me trying to get you into my car. But you'll have your hands full trying to carve out your new position without gossip linking us."

He wheeled the expensive car into the traffic lane. There was only the dim glow of his taillights when the elevator doors opened to allow the first wave of employees into the parking garage.

What did it prove?

Anything? Everything? He was crass enough to bluntly say he wanted to fuck her but reined himself in before he was seen with her.

For his good or hers?

Her fingers suddenly trembled, making it nearly impossible to hold on to her keys. She stumbled into the driver's seat but had to sit for a long time with her fingers curled around the steering wheel.

He'd smelled her?

She should have been mortified. Instead, her arousal twisted deeper inside her, as if it were burrowing into her cells.

It was insane.

The intensity, the savageness of the need so overwhelming, she was actually feeling a little pity for Anastasia.

Well, her pity was probably out of place because she'd just sent him away with a hard cock. Anastasia likely wasn't spending the night alone thanks to her.

Sabra drew in a deep breath and turned on the car. She might be turned on beyond her wildest dreams, but at least she wasn't a complete pushover.

Small comfort really. It would be just her luck to be dreaming about what she'd missed in ten years.

He'd been driving an Aston Martin Vantage.

She made it halfway home before her brain thawed enough for

details to surface. The sun was still up but all she was thinking about were bedroom games.

Okay, with Tarak Nektosha just about anywhere would work. She seemed to have a short circuit when it came to him. Something inside her just punched the panic button and went straight to "get naked"—or more pointedly, "get him naked." She wanted to see his skin, feel it, smell it, lick it. She'd never been so carnal in her life.

Well, she hadn't gotten into the Aston Martin, so that was a point for her. One that came with frustration, but she was working on the sixteenth floor now. Stress was going to be a staple of her diet.

She made a left at the traffic light and entered the neighborhood she lived in. No one owning an Aston Martin would consider it nice, but she was ultra proud of her newly acquired home. It was a three-bedroom, two-story home tucked up against the hills of southern California. Cream stucco decorated the exterior. She slid her sedan into the two-car garage and closed the door.

She'd moved in a year ago with some half-baked idea of Kevin joining her. Tonight, she was eternally grateful she had never asked him to move in. She didn't want any witnesses to just how shaken she was.

What you don't need is a boyfriend to add guilt to the situation…

True. Very, sharply pointedly true.

But it wasn't an issue. She flipped open her phone and reread Kevin's text to reassure herself.

She'd never been so happy about being dumped. Unless she counted her mom, but that wasn't something she needed to think about. Mom was really sort of the wrong word to use for the woman who'd pushed her into the world. Regina Greci hadn't shared her husband's joy over the arrival of their daughter because her plans had only included having a son to impress her father. When Sabra had disappointed her, she'd walked away from both her husband and her newborn daughter the moment she'd recovered from childbirth.

Sabra hit the button for the garage door and walked into her home. It still smelled like new paint, and the walls were pristine. She'd watched the movers like a hawk to make sure they didn't nick the molding. Every cent she had was invested in the place and there was no budget for repairs.

Or furniture. The front room had several pieces in it, but the small family room hidden from the street was completely empty except for an area carpet laid out in front of the fireplace. Kevin had made some comment about it becoming his man cave.

Not in this lifetime.

But getting naked on that carpet with Tarak with nothing but firelight suddenly took hold of her thoughts.

Shit.

She didn't need fantasies of the man cluttering up her new home.

The mail could wait and so could everything else. The only thing she wanted was a shower.

Liar…

Fine, she was a liar, but she still had her pride and a grip on reality. Tarak was in a whole different category of life than she lived in. Sex wouldn't have the same impact on him. She'd be the one nursing injured feelings when he pulled out of her life after satisfying his curiosity.

A long shower really didn't do a whole lot to relieve the ache between her thighs, but her vibrator didn't seem like the right course of action either. Instead, she found herself slipping back into the garter belt.

The only thing she smelled like was soap, but she just couldn't stop thinking about what he'd claimed.

Her musk? It should have sounded lame, but it didn't. Not the way he'd said it, especially when she coupled it with the flash of desire she'd seen in his eyes.

The way the man looked at her was just decadent—as if he was deciding what part of her to taste.

Her clit liked that idea.

It throbbed between the lips of her vagina, her pussy slowly heating back up. The first hint of moisture touched the top of her bare thighs and she caught a hint of her scent. It wasn't unfamiliar, but what was surprising was just how fast she started debating her choice to not get into the convertible.

Her phone rang and she picked it up, grateful for the distraction.

"Did I prove my worth to you?"

She fumbled the phone and it dropped onto the bathroom floor. "Shit." She dove after it and heard Tarak chuckling on the other end.

She could hang up.

Chicken.

She put the phone up to her ear. "Fine, you have integrity. That doesn't mean I plan to… do anything else."

"Pity."

His voice was dark and full of challenge again. Her cheeks darkened in response. The full-length bathroom mirrors gave her a fine view of the physical reaction she was having to him.

"But your front porch is very comfy. Sure you won't come down and join me?"

"You're on my porch?"

He chuckled and ended the call. Her fingers actually turned white because she clutched the phone so tightly. Her master bathroom was in the back of the house, making it impossible to see the porch.

Chicken…

She bit her lower lip in indecision. Hell. Why did he have to be her boss? Her body didn't seem to care. Arousal was burning away inside her and the knowledge that he was a staircase away was just too much temptation. She grabbed a dress and put it on. The top was a crossover and her breasts settled into the cups just fine. Her shoes were still sitting where she'd stepped out of them and she pushed her feet into them before opening the bedroom door.

The expensive sports car looked out of place in her driveway, but Tarak was sprawled in her love seat glider swing as if he were right at home.

Stalking most likely came naturally to him.

Which made opening the front door a stupid idea.

Yet hiding inside was chicken.

"What are you hoping to prove?" she fired off the moment she had the door halfway open.

His lazy stance was a practiced tactic. It had to be, because there was nothing at ease about the look in his eyes. He surveyed her the moment she opened the door, his dark gaze sliding down to the hem of her skirt. His chest rose and fell in a deep motion before his eyes closed halfway.

"You put the garter belt back on."

She crossed her legs in response.

"I just..." Crap. Her tongue felt like a foreign object inside her mouth. His collar was further open, and the front of his shirt was wrinkled from her hands.

Shit. She'd been ready to tear it off him.

And she was heading there again—at breakneck speed.

"You just couldn't stop thinking about it," he finished for her. "About how much you want the same thing I do."

The swing glided back as he stood up. Her porch was suddenly too small. She backed up, right over the threshold, and he followed her. He sent her front door closed with a single push.

"Now there is no one to know we're meeting," he informed her.

"Except for the Aston Martin sitting in my driveway," she argued. "I think that thing is worth as much as my house."

He looked away from her, scanning the small entry that had a double-doorway entrance into the dining room.

"It's worth slightly less." For a split second, he was the man she'd spent the afternoon with, his mind focused on the numbers of the business world. But the moment their eyes met, his glittered with pure intent. "You're redirecting the conversation, Sabra."

He flattened a hand against the wall behind her. She was pinned, without any actual contact between them. But the idea was blazing hot, making her lips tingle with anticipation. The tops of her thighs were slick now, excitement churning away inside her. Her gaze dropped to the front of his pants, any semblance of self-control vanishing.

"I love the way you look at me, Sabra."

She jerked her attention back to his face. Hunger drew his features tight. His eyes flickered with a hunger that just didn't fit inside the civilized suit he'd worn at the office.

"Umm... look, I really can't do this." Her lips were too dry, so she licked them, drawing his dark gaze. "I mean... it's just too damn presumptuous of you to show up on my porch."

He stroked her cheek again, calling attention to the blush stinging her face.

"The word I'd use is *intense*, Sabra." He pressed his thumb over her lower lip, sending a tiny bolt of delight through her. "Something I'm not too sure I like any better than you. My feelings for Anastasia were controllable."

She jerked her head away. "Yeah, you strike me as the sort of man who likes calling the shots."

"Guilty as charged." He leaned forward and hovered over the side of her neck, inhaling deeply. "But that's not what's pissing you off. It's the fact that I told you I'd smelled your pussy."

His words unleashed a riot inside her. She quivered, every muscle joining the revolt against the bindings of self-control. She tried to thrust him away, but all that happened was her hands landed on his chest. Tarak didn't budge.

"I thought women craved honesty. That's what I gave you." He cupped her hip, his grip making her jump. "The question is, are you a big enough girl to deal with me on an honest level? Modern courtship is just bullshit to whitewash the blunt facts of attraction."

"There's a difference between honesty and arrogance."

He slid his hand over the curve of her butt. "Not really. If you won't accept my invitations, boldness is my only option."

Her breath was frozen in her chest for a long moment because part of her just wanted to let him take control. There was no guilt, no need to think when he was the one smashing through her defenses.

But he pushed back, putting a respectable distance between them. "But if you want to play the social-niceties game, I can do that. Where would you like to have dinner?"

The question sounded stupid. Lame. Like something from her high school years.

"Cordial manners don't suit you." The words were out of her mouth before she realized she'd walked right into a trap. His lips curled in victory a moment before his hand was flattened on the wall next to her head once more.

"Finally, the truth," he purred next to her ear. He brushed the side of her neck, sending ripples of sensation down her body before he captured the back of her head again.

He was going to kiss her. She knew it and raised her head even while she was trying to debate the wisdom of allowing it—okay, participating in it. What her brain wanted died in a sizzle as he took command of her lips once more.

But she wanted more than to be kissed. She reached for him, grabbing his shirt again. The fabric bunched up in her hands as she moved her mouth in unison with his. He just tasted good.

And he smelled better.

Everything about him was tactile, basic. She didn't want to be logical; she wanted to be in action.

Her heart was hammering away. Each little pant drew the scent of his skin into her senses. He pressed her mouth open, the tip of his tongue sweeping along her lower lip before probing the interior of her mouth. It was bold and exactly what she expected from him, and she tried to pull him closer.

It wasn't about right or wrong feelings; it was about pure need.

He growled softly, baring his teeth at her before smoothing his hands down her back. Her eyes fluttered shut, his touch delighting her in a way she'd never experienced. She arched, shivering as he cupped her bottom with both hands and squeezed. A jolt of hard need speared through her, making her crazy to have him inside her.

"You're driving me insane, Sabra." Bending over slightly, he kept stroking her until he reached the hem of her skirt, and then he straightened up, smoothing his hands right up the sides of her bare thighs. It was shocking, the contact between their bare skin—so intense, her insides twisted and a little moan rose from her lips.

"That's... that's why... *oh damn it!*... This is too intense." Her voice was a sultry whisper, equal parts need and desperation. "It can't be good for either of us."

His eyes were narrowed to slits. Determination shone from them as he gave her a curt nod. "Maybe," he whispered against her neck before he drew in a deep breath. "But it seems like I just can't resist." He bit her, his teeth grazing her soft skin. Her clit pulsed frantically and she thrust her hips toward his. "Neither can you."

"But I should," she mumbled because her tongue didn't want to form words, only sounds of delight. "You're my boss..."

Her eyelids felt too heavy to lift, but she forced them open. Tarak was watching her, studying her with his sharp gaze. It looked as though he was plotting her downfall.

"I want to taste you."

Her desire vibrated through her as shock numbed her wits.

He scooped her up, cradling her with ease before turning around and depositing her in one of the plush armchairs she had facing into the entryway. One of her shoes dropped to the floor, but she didn't have time to worry about it.

Tarak followed her down, kneeling on the floor in front of her. He flipped her skirt up, and lifted her thighs up to rest on the padded armrests of the chair.

"Tarak… *you can't.*"

He cupped her hips and drew her down to the edge of the chair.

"I like the sound of my name on your lips."

He smoothed a hand across her lower belly. She gasped, her clit pulsing.

"And I love knowing I make you wet."

He rested his hand on her pubic hair for a moment. Anticipation threatened to drive her mad. She was too aroused, too needy to worry about any details. She lifted her hips, seeking out what she craved. It was pure instinct, logic nothing but a burnt cinder now.

He was so damned confident, stroking down through her curls to her slit. She moaned, desperate for release from the churning inside her.

But he didn't finger her. Instead, he separated her folds, opening them to expose her clit. She was so hot, the air felt cold. It was a momentary interruption before he leaned forward and sucked her.

She arched up and off the seat, her thighs clamping around his shoulders. She wasn't close enough and she strained toward him. He didn't tease her. There were no tiny laps from his velvet tongue. Instead, he pressed his tongue straight against her clit and rubbed. Combined with the hot warmth of his mouth, she twisted and burst into climax. There was no control, only the rush of pleasure flooding through her like a wave. It crashed over her, rolling her in its motion before dropping her on the beach in a breathless heap.

"That was fucking sexy," he declared.

"It was stupid." And uncontrolled and in conflict with every idea she had about who she was.

His lips thinned out in response. She tried to scramble up, but he pressed her down with one hand on top of her belly.

"Stupid that I enjoy listening to you come?" There was a hard edge to his voice.

"I just… shouldn't have let you do that."

He responded by thrusting two fingers into her pussy. It shouldn't have felt so good, not after he'd just made her come. But she dug her fingernails into the armrests as her body arched to take him deeper.

"I'm going to watch you come this time."

Damned arrogance. "You shouldn't be so fucking sexy when you're being an arrogant ass." But there was part of her that twisted with anticipation once more. It overrode the impulse to argue with him or insist that her brain resume functioning. The first climax had only whet her appetite for a deeper one.

"And I should have been able to master the urge to drive over here after you told me to get lost in the garage."

His dark eyes glittered with frustration. For a moment, he was the only soul in the world she believed understood how she felt.

"But I didn't." He pumped his fingers inside her, stroking the walls of her passage. It sent waves of delight through her. There was no ignoring it or resisting. "Because I can't get you out of my head, Sabra."

She opened her mouth to argue or maybe agree that they had an insane reaction to one another, but he settled a thumb over her clit and she fell back against the chair as the need to come intensified. The blood was roaring in her ears, and her joints ached because her body was so taut. Nothing mattered except pressing her hips up for the next thrust. The orgasm was centered deep inside her this time, every thrust of his fingers touching it until it burst.

She cried out this time, no soft exclamation of delight but a full shout borne of rapture. It was hard, jerking her entire body before dropping her back into reality. She was panting when her brain decided to work again. When she opened her eyes, she stared into Tarak's. Satisfaction appeared in those midnight orbs before he stood up.

"I'm not going to fuck you."

Her muscles were lax, making any sort of movement difficult. He pulled a handkerchief from his pocket and dried his fingers.

"I'm leaving now, because if I don't, I will end up fucking you."

He cupped her cheek and kissed her gently before straightening up and reaching for the doorknob.

"But... I don't understand."

He paused with the door open. The evening breeze blew against him, depressing the front of his trousers to show her the outline of his erection.

"I'm leaving to prove I do have integrity. When you let me between your thighs, you're going to make the decision with your wits clear."

She pushed her skirt down, her temper rising. "You mean you're leaving because you're afraid to let me see you lose control."

His face tightened. "Maybe." His knuckles turned white around the doorknob. "Good night, Sabra."

He passed through the door and closed it firmly behind him.

Chicken...

The Aston Martin roared to life as she drew in a deep breath. She wanted to scream at him but refused to chase him.

Nope, she wasn't going after him.

The sound of the car began to diminish into the distance.

Good.

But it wasn't good. She shivered, feeling exposed and vulnerable. It was acute and her emotions suddenly became so tender, tears made her eyes glassy. She pulled her legs up and hugged them. The soft beach colors she'd used to decorate her entry room failed to soothe her. She'd never felt so abandoned, and it tore at the fabric of everything she believed. There was nothing about her dealings with Tarak that fit into her choices about the life she was going to have.

She responded to him without thought, and she didn't even have the solace of knowing it was alcohol induced.

Sobering up wasn't going to save her.

Chapter 3

"Claudia is your secretary, along with three other Junior VPs."

"Good morning, Ms. Donovan," Claudia said with a sweet smile on her face. "Coffee?"

"When we've finished her introduction tour," the head of security informed the secretary.

Claudia bobbed her head in response. Her desk was positioned between four identical glass doors.

Mr. Kim didn't miss a step as he led Sabra through to her office. The guy moved with a fluid grace that spoke of just how much of a badass he likely was if you gave him a reason to show you. He had Asian features and black hair that was cut back to just a quarter inch.

No one would be using a handful of that against him in a fight.

"This will be your office."

Her office...

It was frickin' unreal.

"For the moment your title is unclear," Mr. Kim continued. "You are attached to the marketing department at the VP level. Mr. Nektosha will be meeting with the senior project managers to decide which projects your education and experience might fit."

He extended an arm toward her desk. A neat stack of papers was laid out on the smooth, black, glass surface. "You'll need to sign a new confidentiality agreement, which includes a declaration of allegiance to the country since you will have access to defense contract details. Your security code will be activated once you return those to me. And I'll tell Claudia you prefer tea."

"How did you know that?"

It really wasn't the best question she could have asked. It lacked a lot—a whole frickin' lot considering she was being shown her new office on the sixteenth floor. She should be more polished, more confident. Instead, she sounded like a teenager being confronted by her parents when she came in late after a date.

Mr. Kim didn't even blink as he answered her.

"Security is always a prime concern here at Nektosha. No matter what floor. New employees are always observed and I read your file an hour ago."

He disappeared behind the dark, frosted glass wall that separated her from Claudia.

Her secretary.

She wanted to giggle like a little girl in her princess dress, but there was one thing more important. She sat down and began to read the contracts. Her fingers itched to just grab a pen and sign, but that was unprofessional. She would start her new job the way she intended to do it, by checking the details and making sure it was done right.

This was her chance and she wasn't afraid of proving herself. She was eager to dive into the new position. True to his word, Glen enabled her employee identification number the moment he received her contracts. The computer on her desk became a portal to understanding Nektosha Industries.

The company was as amazing as its owner. They were more than just solvent; she checked the numbers twice because it didn't seem possible for them to be doing so well in the current economic climate.

Her intercom buzzed. She looked up and pressed the key to allow Claudia to speak with her.

"Will there be anything else, Ms. Donovan?"

A quick glance at the time told her the day was gone.

"Um… no. Thanks."

Sabra killed the intercom and realized her neck was stiff.

Her first day on the sixteenth floor, and she'd loved it so much, she hadn't even looked at the clock.

She flexed her arms and stretched her back before pulling her purse out of the lower desk drawer. Her cell phone started chiming at exactly two minutes after five.

"Do I need an appointment to see you now?" her best friend Celeste purred on the other end of the line. Celeste had an unfair advantage against the rest of the female population. She was gorgeous, gorgeous, and utterly gorgeous.

"Agree to wear a chador and it's a date."

There was a husky laugh on the other end of the phone. "You're going to swell my head, Sabra. You are not that hard on the eyes."

"When I stand next to you, I look like a baby parrot, fresh from the egg."

"That makes it vital that you meet me at Angelino's. You need pasta to fill out your plumage."

"Somehow, I don't think that's what will fill out," Sabra remarked dryly. She was starving but had burned maybe a hundred calories at her desk all day.

Celeste laughed and cut the line. Sabra made sure her computer was off before heading toward the door. A prickle of sensation tingled down her nape as she neared it. She hadn't really been hiding. Besides, Tarak wasn't the type to be deterred by an office door.

Maybe he was serious about keeping their relationship out of the workplace.

Well, that might sound good if they were having anything that could be called a relationship.

Which they weren't.

He'd wrung her like a wet dish towel and left her. It was undermining her confidence, because everything she'd decided she wanted didn't seem to make much impact when she was near the man. Impulse ruled completely.

And he didn't want to let her do the same to him.

That suited him completely. He had a lot in common with his ancestors. The Apache had held out longer than any other tribe. Tarak took what he wanted and guarded himself against what he didn't care for.

For a moment, she was lost in a daydream of what she might be able to reduce him to—maybe it was because she wanted vengeance or maybe she wanted to soothe her pride by proving he had as many soft spots as she did.

So she hadn't really tried to rock his world yet, but he'd maintained such tight control of her, she hadn't had the chance. She knew without a doubt that it was by design. It was a facet of his character, the controlling urge that often came off as arrogant. It was sexy as hell, but frustrating too. The urge to try her hand at reducing him to the same state he'd left her in was growing stronger, the challenge of it addictive. Sex had never been a competitive sport for her before. She got the feeling Tarak preferred sex that way.

She shivered.

Before groaning.

It was definitely time for a girls' night.

Claudia was gone and the outer hallway was empty. It was impossible to tell if there was anyone else still working, but she still glanced down to the end of the hallway, where Tarak's office took up an entire side of the floor. His secretary normally sat at a desk outside, making it look even more formidable.

But there was no one there.

Which was best. After the launch was finished, he tended to disappear. It was the reason she'd not really known what he looked like. Tarak preferred the test and development track office up in Anchorage. Of course, he was a hands-on man, a recluse with a multibillion-dollar company. Finding a willing bed partner wouldn't be hard. She'd had her chance.

It was stupid to feel disappointed, but she couldn't dismiss the feeling as it swept through her.

Angelino's was sounding better and better.

Traffic was a bitch, but it was the price one paid for living near the west shoreline. Cars passed her with girls in bikini tops on their way in from a day on the sand. Angelino's overlooked the surf and had prices to reflect their high-class location.

It didn't matter; she was celebrating.

She pulled up to the front and a valet opened her door. She pressed a five-dollar bill into his hand in the vain hope he would keep her car from getting scratched. If there was a bad parking place, she was likely to get it before the convertibles some of the clientele were arriving in.

Celebrating…

"So what's the title?" Celeste had her long legs crossed as she waited on a leather sofa inside. She stood up, balancing perfectly on her spike heels.

"No title until they decide which project I'm getting."

Celeste pushed her lips into a pout.

"But there is a secretary."

Her friend bestowed a smile on her. The hostess guided them through the restaurant. Men looked up as Celeste passed, but she didn't give them even a glance. She was grace in motion, her trim figure complemented by sweet features. Her blond hair was so light it was almost white, giving her a fae appearance.

The hostess stopped at a window seat. A waiter appeared to pull out a chair for Celeste. "Compliments of the manager, Ms. Connor."

Celeste sat down and smiled at the hostess. But the moment

she'd handed them their menus, Celeste was back on the hunt for more details.

"A private secretary?" She clicked her fingernails together delicately. "Very nice. I'm sure we need some wine to commemorate the moment."

A waiter was hovering and produced a wine list. The man hovered over Celeste, grinning like a teenager on prom night when she smiled at him. But once their wine was corked and poured, her friend was focused on her again.

Sabra lifted her glass and watched the sunset turn the white wine scarlet. "It was quite a day. Thanks for inviting me out."

"Yes, well, we have two things to celebrate," Celeste declared softly. "Your promotion and the so very overdue kicking to the curb of one Kevin Guterman."

Celeste winkled her perfect little nose as she mispronounced Kevin's last name to make it sound like *gutter*.

Sabra pointed at her. "Don't go starting that now. My taste in men isn't any worse than yours."

Celeste leaned to one side, exposing the slim column of her neck. Two men at the table beside them looked over at her like hungry hounds. Celeste smiled slowly before cutting them a quick glance that sent one of their forks clattering onto the dinnerware.

"You are such a bitch," Sabra laughed.

"Then she's in good company."

Sabra jerked her head around to see Anastasia glaring at her. She blinked but only had a moment to confirm that it was in fact Tarak's discarded pet standing over her. Anastasia struck fast and hard, taking a swing at Sabra. Pain exploded on the side of Sabra's face before she managed to shove Anastasia away from her. The table wobbled and the wine went spilling onto the floor.

Anastasia squealed as Celeste very neatly pinned her arm behind her back. For all her innocent looks, Celeste was a talented martial artist. Anastasia thrashed like a freshly caught fish but was powerless to escape.

"Tarak Nektosha is mine—" Anastasia panted as two waiters began to haul her out of the restaurant. "Mine, you slut!"

"Ladies, I apologize for the disturbance." The owner of the voice sent the staff scrambling to clean up the table. "I'm Nartan Lupan, the owner. Please allow me to reseat you."

Sabra was mopping wine off her skirt and looked up. Nartan was exactly like his restaurant—posh and upscale. He had cobalt-blue eyes that looked as keen as a hawk's.

He extended his arm toward a set of sliding doors. Beyond them was the private, members' only section of Angelino's, a place Sabra had never seen the inside of. Even if her pride wanted to balk, her curiosity wasn't going to let her toss away the opportunity.

"Thank you."

Sabra was already moving toward the doors when she realized Celeste was frozen. She was staring at Nartan, her perfect complexion darkening with a blush. She stiffened and hurried to catch Sabra. The staff slid the doors closed behind them, shutting out the noise from the dining room. Here there was the sound of the surf and soft music, and this side of the building was comprised of arched doorways, currently open to the summer night.

"My sincerest apologies, ladies. I hope you will enjoy your dinner," Nartan continued. He reached into his jacket and withdrew a business card. "Please feel free to call me anytime you wish to dine at Angelino's."

He offered the card to Celeste. Sabra's normally polished sidekick hesitated. It looked as if she had to force herself to take the card and she only held it by the corner.

"Thank you," Sabra spoke up. Nartan flashed her a grin before striding off.

"Are you all right, Celeste?"

Her friend shivered but shook her head. "Of course I am." She dropped the card onto the table, facedown. She took a deep breath before reaching for a wineglass some waiter had already filled. She took a sip before composing herself.

"Now tell me why Tarak Nektosha's name is being linked with yours by that gold digger?"

Sabra reached for her own wineglass. "It's all part of the tale of how I managed to make it to the sixteenth floor."

Celeste watched her over the rim of her glass as she began the story.

"I will take care of Anastasia," Tarak Nektosha informed his friend.

Nartan held his cell phone to his ear as he watched his private guests through a one-way mirror. "You sound ominous, my friend, a passion normally lacking in your liaisons."

"Don't pry, Nartan. Right now I'm ready to thank you for calling me up."

"So don't piss you off by noticing the tone of your voice?" Nartan observed smugly.

There was a pause on the other end of the phone. "Exactly."

Nartan chuckled. "The little raven is quite fetching. She looks like she purrs—under the right touch of course."

"She's mine."

Nartan aimed his gaze at Sabra, but her companion distracted him once again. "As much as I enjoy giving you competition that will make you sweat, in this case, I find her friend far more to my liking."

"Glad to hear it," Tarak spoke softly. "And send them a bottle of ice wine, with my compliments."

Nartan put his phone back in his pocket and gestured his head waiter over.

"Ice wine for the ladies."

The waiter went to see to it.

Everyone in the private section was linked to money somehow, even if it was as simple as whose bed they were warming. But there was something different about Sabra and her companion. Nartan watched as his waiter brought the bottle of ice wine over for their approval. Sabra Donovan turned red as she pushed her lips into a pout.

He chuckled and pulled his phone back out. Tarak picked up on the first ring.

"The look on her face says she isn't yours, my friend."

Tarak snarled something profane. "She will be."

And the line went dead.

───※───

"Explain that look, Sabra Marie Donovan, and thank God it is not about to become Guterman," Celeste demanded the moment the waiter left the table.

"It's nothing."

Celeste laughed and leaned across the table. "It looked like a whole lot of something naughty that you're not comfortable with."

"I'm not doing my boss," Sabra defended herself.

"Your boss... Interesting," Celeste purred victoriously. "It sounds like you're trying to convince yourself of that fact."

Heat teased Sabra's cheeks, and she had to bite back the cuss word she wanted to say. Celeste always saw straight through her.

"Okay, fine. He's a hunk—"

"Who is?" Celeste asked innocently.

"Can the eyelash flutters. Remember, I know where your skeletons are stashed."

Celeste lifted a single, slim finger. "That is a two-way street."

It was. They'd been friends since grade school. Sabra picked up the glass of ice wine and inhaled its scent. It brought Tarak to mind instantly. She shivered before setting the glass down.

"Now I really have to know what is happening between you and Tarak Nektosha," Celeste declared. "You actually look shaken."

"Like you did when Nartan offered you his card?"

Celeste lifted her glass and took a sip. "Touché." She set her glass down and appeared to steady herself. "Yet my situation is easier to understand. You know why I don't trust men."

For a moment Celeste was locked in a memory. Her eyes became wounded as she recalled her ex-husband. Sabra remembered the asshole too well, but it was a lot easier for her to discard the memory. She hadn't been the one living with a monster. Celeste was caught in the moment, so Sabra spoke up to shatter the hold the past had on her friend.

"Well, I don't trust Tarak Nektosha," Sabra confessed. "I mean, how did he know we were here?"

Celeste sighed. "Men with money always look out for one another." She picked up the card Nartan had given her and held it over the candle flame. "Their allegiance is to the boys' club." The paper caught and a yellow flame greedily consumed the card. Celeste watched it burn before dropping it into her water glass. "We are pets to their sort, nothing more. Which is why *we* must look out for one another," Celeste finished softly, but not too soft for Sabra to hear the determination in her tone.

·······

No matter how good the reason for celebrating was, it was still a work night. Sabra hugged Celeste before getting into her car and heading home. Traffic was much lighter and she was soon pulling into her driveway.

But she shivered when she entered the house. It was quiet, but the whisper of a memory sent a ripple of sensation across her skin.

A memory of Tarak.

The house phone was ringing and she looked at the caller ID.

"Hey, Dad."

"Where have you been?" her father asked. "I've left five messages."

"You should have called me on my cell."

"That's your office line," her father admonished. "When I was in the navy, we never used the base phone."

"That was a few years ago, Dad."

"Values don't go out of style."

"Yeah, Dad." Sabra kicked her shoes off. "I know the family motto."

There was an approving grunt on the other end of the phone. But the ice wine and Tarak's words from the meeting joined her father's argument. Her boss could track her anywhere and even see the little text message from Kevin.

"I'm going to get a private cell phone, Dad. Promise. First thing Saturday."

"It sounds like there have been developments in your career if there is budget for a cell phone."

She turned around and leaned against the kitchen counter. Her dad was her best friend, the parent who had wanted her. Sure, she was grown and past childhood insecurities, but her mother's desertion still had the power to hurt. Her dad's voice soothed the wounds. He'd launched into a tale of his navy years and she laughed again, as she had the hundred other times she'd heard the same story.

"All right, off to bed with you, young lady," her father said at last. "Story time is over."

"Not until you tell me what the doctor said today."

There was a short silence on the other end of the phone.

"Dad, I'm not going to be brushed off that easily," she warned him. "I was raised by a crusty sailor."

Her father offered her a chuckle. "You're my girl, through and through. The doctor told me to get a second opinion if I didn't like what he had to say. So that's what I'm doing."

"Dad—"

"That's my plan, Sabra. I'm a grown man, and I've lived enough years to know that one doctor doesn't always agree with another one. Now you sleep tight and I'll call you tomorrow."

Her dad was so damned stubborn.

Just like Tarak.

The man was also insanely vibrant; his essence was floating through her house. Wasn't there some unspoken law of the universe that made it impossible to be turned on while talking to your father? It didn't seem to be applying itself. The darkness just made her long for companionship even more.

——

The feeling followed her into her bedroom and sleep eluded her. At least good, sound sleep did. She was grateful for her alarm putting an end to her tossing. But one look in the mirror and she knew the day was going to be a bitch.

The right side of her face was black and blue. She rubbed her eyes and looked again, hoping she was just groggy.

No such luck.

Anastasia had clobbered her good. Maybe Celeste had the right idea—a few martial arts lessons might just be the ticket. At least the idea kept her moving and got her to work on time.

"Good morning, Ms—" Claudia covered her gaping mouth with her hand.

"It's not as bad as it looks." Sabra tried to make her tone light.

"Yes it is."

Recognition was instant. It felt as if she registered Tarak's voice on a cellular level. He was standing in the hallway, holding the door she'd just come through open. His suit was Armani and his shirt pressed perfectly. He looked like a corporate tycoon, until she locked gazes with him. Once she looked into his eyes, all she saw was the

Apache. There was nothing about him that fit in with the society around them.

"My office, Ms. Donovan. We need to discuss last evening."

She avoided making eye contact until she was inside his office. As far as business tycoon dens went, it was cutting edge, but she was still dwelling on the fact that he'd known where she was the night before.

She was only two steps inside his office when she demanded, "Are we alone?"

He whipped around, his hair flipping back from his face. "Yes."

"Then this better be about business and not the bruise your girlfriend left on my face."

He didn't like her statement, not a bit. But he just crossed his arms over his chest and leaned against the edge of his desk, which was gigantic and impressive. But she was concentrating on his reasons for dragging her into his office while letting his secretary hear that he was keeping tabs on her after hours.

"You told me that I am up here because you think I can handle the job. Saying you want to discuss last night in front of both our secretaries isn't keeping this on a professional level."

His gaze settled on the side of her face. "You're right, but the situation is extreme."

"It's a bruise and I've had worse."

A ghost of a smile touched his lips. She got stuck looking at his mouth. God, he knew how to kiss. Kevin sure hadn't curled her toes the way Tarak did.

"Now who's thinking about non-business topics, Ms. Donovan?"

She jerked her attention up and found his black eyes glittering. He'd pushed away from the desk and closed the distance between them. Great. She'd given him an inch and he was taking full advantage.

But she had to confess that she'd be disappointed if he didn't, even though her pride rebelled against the thought. Emotion and fact often conflicted. On one level, she wanted to be viewed as his peer—on another, deeper one, she wanted to be stalked.

And caught...

He stopped in front of her, reaching out to tip her head away just a bit so he could inspect the bruise. His lips thinned with rage.

"Anastasia is back in New York." He stroked her cheek gently. "I put her on the damned plane myself."

"You did what with her?" The words flew right out of her mouth in the same moment it registered that he'd confessed to being with the sex kitten.

Tarak's expression instantly changed. He hadn't missed the heat in her tone. He cupped her jaw, raising her face so that their gazes couldn't part.

"I put her on a plane so that her father can deal with her. I want nothing else from her."

His tone was sharp and cold as ice. There wasn't a shred of remorse for his actions.

Sabra stepped back, escaping from his touch. "Not that it's any of my concern."

"You are jealous, Sabra."

He took a step after her. A crazy twist of excitement went through her as she realized he was stalking her. Intent flickered in his eyes as he took another step.

She retreated. Moved back, without any real decision on her part. Tarak's eyes narrowed and he followed her. Arousal snaked through her and her mouth went dry. It was too damned fast to make any sort of sense.

"Very jealous," he concluded as he shortened the space between them. "I approve."

"Why? You're the one who prefers relationships you are in command of. I thought you said Anastasia fit that bill perfectly, so that makes her a better choice for you. I don't do the no-strings-attached thing."

Sabra sidestepped, because she was running out of space behind her. A picture of him pressing her up against the wall was trying to destroy every last shred of sense she had left.

"Sure you want to discuss what I like in a relationship, Sabra? Because once I get interested in a project, I tend to see it through to my complete satisfaction," he warned.

Her mouth went dry at the mention of *satisfaction*.

"It's not like I want to. This whole instant-attraction thing isn't my idea of a good time. In fact, I'm over it."

She was such a liar...

His expression tightened, determination flickering in his eyes. "Like hell you're over it." His lazy pace had given her a false sense of security, of control over the situation. The brutal truth was, she had none. Tarak reached out and captured her, pulling her against his body as he turned and pushed her up against the dark, frosted-glass wall.

"When you issue a challenge to me, Sabra, rest assured, I will take it."

He caught the back of her head and angled his face so that he could kiss her. His mouth was hot, and once again her toes curled. Desire was instantaneous with the first touch of his lips against hers, as if she'd been waiting until they were once again in contact. Being pinned against a wall only made the moment more intense. He handled her as though she belonged to him, and part of her wanted it to be true.

She reached for him, for the hair that drew her gaze every time he was near, tangling her fingers in the longer strands to pull him closer. He was pressing her against the wall, but they weren't close enough. She lifted her leg, hooking it around his hip. He stroked her thigh and cupped her bottom as his tongue thrust deep inside her mouth. Her skirt rode up, allowing the inside of her thigh to rub against his hip. He shifted, pressing against her pubic mound. The hard presence of his cock sent a twist of need through her.

"Goddamn it," he swore, and pressed his forehead against the glass wall. His breathing was rapid and the grip on her butt tightened as if he was fighting the urge to release her. The layers of fabric between them were a torment from hell.

"I want inside you, Sabra." He shoved away from the wall with a vicious action that sent a vibration up the glass panel.

"It's fucking consuming me, and I don't have time for emotional distractions. I should have taken care of the urge when I was at your house."

He moved away, shaking his head as if he was desperate to get her out of his mind. She lowered her leg, feeling exposed and naïve.

Too damned vulnerable.

"Well, excuse the hell out of me."

There was venom in her tone and her temper flared. She let it run wild, needing something to burn off the passion trying to make her knees buckle.

He whipped around, but she beat him to the punch.

"Don't you touch me again. Maybe you're sex on a stick and hotter than any man I've ever had in my bed, but at least my last boyfriend wasn't such an egomaniac that sex was only about him. I've got higher standards than being fucked out of your system."

She opened the door, but it was slammed shut with a violence that shook the entire wall. He was only an inch from her back, and she could feel his body heat. His scent filled her nose, sending a stabbing bolt of need through her. His greater size overwhelmed her and turned up the heat burning her another few degrees. There was something about the way he demanded what he wanted that was sexy as sin, and it sent a shiver down her spine.

"I deserved that," he admitted next to her ear.

"Yeah?" She turned around and shoved him. "Then why do you sound like those were the hardest words you've ever spoken?"

He caught her wrists, clamping them in an iron grip.

"Because they were. This is my domain—the gain, the risk, it's all mine. I don't apologize for telling people what I want. I am Nektosha. If you come into my world, be prepared to satisfy me."

He pressed all the way against her, the contact sending her blood racing.

But the intercom buzzed, filling the office. "Mr. Nektosha?" The Asian security chief's voice cut through the office. "Is there a problem?"

"No, Kim. Close the intercom."

There was a quick buzz, confirming exactly what he'd claimed—it was his world. There was an undeniable allure about him, but it was the same sort of fascination she might have for a snake. The attraction stemmed from the danger, and the reality was, she was likely to end up the victim. She sighed and tried to twist her wrists free.

"Better patch things up with Anastasia then, because I will not jump into your bed on command."

"You've never tried my commands in bed." He leaned down and kissed the side of her neck. "Sometimes, hearing what your partner wants is very stimulating."

His voice was dark and bold. Her knees went weak again as his cock pressed against her belly. She trembled with need so intense, she bit her lip to contain the little telltale sound that wanted to rise from her chest.

"Be in the parking garage at ten to five."

"No." It took every bit of self-control she had to deny what she wanted so badly.

He moved so that he was hovering over her lips, but she turned her face. He growled, low and dangerously.

"Why not?"

"Because I am not Anastasia. You don't tell me where and when to make myself available for your sexual needs."

"Your needs too, Sabra." He drew in a deep breath next to her neck before lifting his head and locking gazes with her. "You're wet and quivering with desire. *For me.*"

He backed up, running a hand through his hair. "I promised you I'd keep this out of the office. So be in the garage."

So simple, yet so devoid of emotion too.

Frustration was driving her insane. Her body was a mass of impulses, all of them doing their best to overwhelm her better judgment. She closed her hand into a fist and squeezed until her fingernails bit into her palms.

"Sorry, I don't do casual sex." She couldn't stop the small smile that curved her lips. "Even if the offer is tempting."

She drew herself up and started to turn her back on him. But he reached out and caught her chin with his thumb and forefinger.

"There will be nothing casual about it."

There was a dark promise in his voice, one she was sure she was going to hear in her dreams for a really long time. But she shook his hold off and turned her back on him.

"Now who's trying to control their sexual encounters?" he shot at her back.

She turned and sent him a hard look. "It's called being wary. You want something completely different than I do."

He shook his head. "We both want to get naked and fuck. Call me what you will, but you will not label me dishonest. I want to get between your thighs and I've got the balls to say it. You had your leg around my hip because you wanted me inside you just as badly as I wanted to be there. You're the one who can't call a spade a spade."

He sat down at his desk, dismissing her.

He had a point. She was trying to mold the attraction between them into something sweeter. The hard fact was, she wanted to jump his bones and didn't really care about anything else when she was around him.

It was humiliating to want him so badly that she was willing to skip past even a hint of a budding relationship. He'd be lightning to ride—she didn't doubt it. What she truly questioned was her ability to walk away. It was fun to think of herself as that sophisticated, but the truth was, she doubted her heart was at freezing temperature—or at least cold enough for her to report to work on the same floor with him after he decided she was out of his system.

Tarak's heart was that cold though.

Which was why she walked out of his office without a backward glance. He was everything she expected of a billion-dollar tycoon. Every action was razor-sharp. The intensity was normal for him, but she was pretty sure it was going to eat her alive.

So she walked away.

—⁓—

The day flew by too fast. Funneling her attention into impressing Tarak on a professional level kept her from dwelling on the fact that he had a point.

She was being dishonest.

But she was also her father's daughter, and her daddy was right—values didn't go out of style.

It sucked.

Seriously sucked.

The facts were polar opposite to what she felt. It was all churning around inside her. When she left work, going home felt like some sort of surrender. She didn't want to be predictable. Part of her wanted Tarak to guess where she was, to continue their stalking game, and he wouldn't be doing that so long as she carried around a work phone with a location chip inside it.

That thought gave her an impulse that had nothing to do with the way her boss turned her on. Sabra made a left turn and headed toward a strip mall. The rush-hour traffic was creeping along as the warm California sun set. She pulled smoothly into a parking place and entered the cell phone store. A fresh-faced kid with glasses greeted her.

Okay, it was just a cell phone, but an hour later she was immensely pleased with her efforts. At least until she realized that she was still just as hung up on her boss.

Total suckage.

Anastasia showed up in her dreams.

Sabra watched the blond coming closer while she was paralyzed, seeing the manicured fingernails with amazing clarity. Anastasia raised her fist and brought it down while Sabra lost the battle to contain her cry.

She jerked awake, sitting up.

Her bedroom was dark except for the splinters of light making their way through her closed blinds. The streetlamps outside her window burned all night long. It had been a nuisance when she first moved in, but tonight she enjoyed having just enough light to gain her bearings. Her forehead was wet with perspiration and her heart was thumping hard.

It really pissed her off too.

Anastasia didn't rate high enough for nightmares.

At least she shouldn't.

A glance at the clock told her it was three in the morning. With a huff, she turned onto her side and tried to go back to sleep. But she made the mistake of choosing her bruised side and ended up jerking away from her pillow when pain sliced through her.

Maybe it was time to take Celeste up on her offer to teach her some self-defense moves.

"Good morning, Ms. Donovan." Claudia flashed her a bright smile. "I'll get your morning tea."

"Thanks."

It still felt a little awkward to be on the command end of a working relationship, but the moment Sabra sat down at her computer and logged in, she realized she didn't have time to get a cup of tea. Her inbox was full and her internal messaging system was lit up like a Christmas tree. Life on the sixteenth floor was going to be a hustle. Now that she had a project to manage, she was getting a quick education as to why no one on the lower floors ever saw the VPs. It was because they were all chained to their desks.

The sheer level of work waiting for her attention almost made her feel guilty for how harshly she'd thought about those VPs for ignoring the calls on a Saturday night. It looked as though free time was going to become precious. Very precious.

It also made Tarak's cut-to-the-bedroom attitude on sex a little easier to understand. Being a successful business tycoon probably didn't leave a lot of time for long walks on the beach.

But that wasn't what she wanted from him anyway.

Claudia delivered the tea as Sabra was trying to sort through the internal messages.

"Your morning meetings have changed because Mr. Nektosha has left."

Sabra looked up instantly. Too fast really, but Claudia didn't notice; she was on her way out already.

Left?

She bit her lip, trying to tell herself it didn't bother her. She failed, but at least ended up with the notion that it was for the best.

By the end of the day, she was mentally exhausted from the struggle not to think about it. It was quite possible she'd have spent less energy if she'd just let her disappointment surface.

Someone from accounting turned to stare at her in the parking garage, surprise appearing on her face as she got a good look at the bruise still darkening Sabra's eye. The woman turned away quickly, but it was enough to remind Sabra of her nightmare.

She dug out the business card Celeste had given her and punched the address into her navigation system. It was a long overdue visit. Martial arts training was the one thing they hadn't shared.

The martial arts school Celeste taught at was a direct opposite to her stylish friend. Sabra looked at the business card twice to make sure she was at the right place. The strip mall was a decade out of date. Sabra was sure Celeste didn't have a pair of shoes that was three years old.

The first step inside made her pause. The place smelled like sweat, pure and simple. There was a long seating area with a collection of mothers sitting in groups. Most of them were playing with their cell phones as a group of young students practiced in front of them. Every one of the kids wore a white uniform. They had different colored belts and were quick to snap to attention when the instructor gave them commands. He was using a pair of padded training paddles that popped when he hit them together. A fan was blowing back and forth in the far corner, but the air was still stale.

"May I help you?"

Another man had come out of an office. A tattered black belt was knotted around his waist. His uniform was red, but it was the threadbare condition of his belt that impressed her the most. The guy spent a lot of hours with it on. He was of Asian descent with a warm honey skin tone and black hair.

"Yes, I think I want to try some self-defense classes."

⸻

"You're going to hurt tomorrow."

Celeste's uniform was wet in places and her hair slicked back with perspiration. It was the most disheveled Sabra had seen her bombshell buddy in years.

"So will you."

Celeste sent her a smile that was bright with victory. "It's a pain I like, and it's addictive." She stared at the bruise on the side of Sabra's face. "You'll see."

There was a tone in her voice that made Sabra reach over and hug her. Celeste laughed softly at her.

"I'm fine, Sabra. Better than fine. I'm great, because I've chosen to be."

Sabra gave her friend a hard look. "When is Caspian due out of prison?"

Celeste shrugged but didn't quite pull off the nonchalant gesture. "He has plenty of friends who could come after me if he wanted vengeance."

"He's playing the good boy for the benefit of the parole board."

Celeste's expression hardened. "No doubt, but I refuse to think about him. He isn't worth it." She clicked her car remote and the taillights flashed on her Corvette. "Why couldn't you and I be lesbians again? We have so much in common."

"Because we're both pathetically strictly dick." Sabra reminded her.

Celeste shook her head and pulled open the door of her car. She slid behind the wheel of the stylish sports car with a natural grace that should have been illegal after the hours they'd been training.

Sabra collapsed into the driver's seat of her sedan, grateful to be off her feet. Her butt hurt and so did her legs. Her back felt as if it were going to be on fire in the morning, but she still wasn't sorry she'd pushed to stay for a second class. Tae kwon do was going to be like everything else in her life—being average wasn't going to cut it for her. She wanted to be at the top and that meant pushing herself. It meant facing challenges.

Alone in the car, she had no energy left to ignore how much

Tarak Nektosha was testing her resolve—or that she'd turned her back on the challenge he presented. Oh sure, she'd done it for all the right reasons—noble reasons, moral ones that didn't change how frustrated she was with how brief their moments had been. Even with him gone, she felt like she was waiting for his return. It was a dangerous little feeling, one that might grow strong enough to strangle her if she didn't clip it fast.

Not that she really had to do anything.

The man was gone. Sure, he'd be back, but she doubted he'd be interested in her. Men like him didn't spend their time trying to rekindle fires that hadn't given them what they wanted.

—◦◦◦—

"Should I fire my chef?" Nartan asked. "Or just save you from yourself by calling that little raven up?"

Angelino's was full, but the private dining room was empty except for Tarak and Nartan. Even the staff was sealed behind a soundproof, clear door. Nartan got five grand a night for the exclusive table with a balcony view of the Pacific Ocean.

"She works for me," Tarak growled. "I can call her if I want to."

Nartan took a sip from a tumbler of whisky. His features tightened as the strong liquor slid across his tongue. "You want to," he decided. "A little too much, which is why you are sitting here, growling."

Tarak lifted his middle finger and sent his friend a single-finger salute.

Nartan offered him a toast. "Cussing me out won't change anything."

"What does that mean?"

Nartan swirled the whisky around the glass for a long moment. "It means you came to see me because you know I won't kiss your ass and avoid mentioning the elephant in the room." He looked up, locking stares with Tarak. A lifetime of events locked them together in a brotherhood that was the closest thing to family either of them had. "Or in this case, the shadow of a little raven in your eyes. You're thinking about her."

"I need to stop." Tarak reached for his own whisky but only curled his fingers around the glass. It wasn't what he craved. "She works for me."

"Your unbendable rules getting in the way?"

Tarak nodded. "How many of your waitresses have you banged?"

"None," Nartan confirmed. "I never said I didn't agree with you, only that it's clear you're thinking about her. Her shadow is following you."

"We've been off the reservation a little too long for that crap."

"Fine." Nartan lifted his glass and held it in the air between them. "Toss that double back, call one of those friends with benefits you have, and deal with the heat making you edgy. It's not like I haven't seen you do it before."

"You've done the same."

Nartan nodded curtly. "I'm not the one who's torn tonight."

Tarak didn't respond. He sipped at the whisky until the tumbler was empty. "You're right."

Nartan lifted an eyebrow in question.

"I am torn." Tarak stood up and walked out onto the balcony. The wind blew his hair back, rushing down the open collar of his shirt.

Torn, but he knew without a doubt he didn't want anyone but Sabra. So he watched the moon rise over the Pacific Ocean, remaining on the balcony by sheer force of will.

The fascination wouldn't last. Nothing with a woman ever did.

Chapter 4

"HAVE A NICE WEEKEND, Ms. Donovan." Claudia smiled before lifting her purse and heading toward the elevators.

Sabra hesitated in the doorway of her office. Now that it was the end of the week, she felt like she'd passed a milestone. Security hadn't shown up to escort her downstairs and out the door, and she was almost sure that two of the VPs had decided to like her.

The weekend was almost unwelcome because it was going to interrupt her climb to being a respected member of the team. But she wasn't going to go so far as to say that she was going to miss her alarm going off in the morning.

She turned the music up as she drove home, singing along with the tune until she turned the corner onto her block. The Aston Martin Vantage was back in her driveway.

A ripple of anticipation traveled along her skin. She didn't pull into the double garage because keeping him out of her personal space seemed wiser. He was bold enough to walk right in if the door was up. Instead, she pulled into the driveway and stepped out of her car.

She thought she was ready to face him, but her belly twisted with excitement the moment she laid eyes on Tarak. He was on the double-glider seat again, his shirt collar open and the knot of his necktie pulled down several inches. His legs were stretched out and crossed at the ankles.

"If you need to see me, you can call me into your office, Mr. Nektosha."

She managed to control her tone and sound smooth even though she fell a little short of chilly professionalism.

"If you're too afraid to be alone with me, Ms. Donovan, by all means, admit it."

His verbal sparring skills were just as cutthroat as the rest of his abilities. She fingered her keys, realizing that the ball was very much in her court. "Please come in."

It felt like inviting a vampire into her home. Once the invitation was past her lips, she was going to lose all control of the situation. She turned the key in the lock and pushed the door open. She turned around and watched Tarak follow her.

He wasn't the commitment sort of guy, so there was no reason for her to be so melodramatic.

But he paused and looked at the chair in her living room. Heat teased her cheeks as her clit throbbed.

"I told you at the office I wasn't interested in the sort of relationship you want." She put her purse down. "Why are you here?"

He shifted his gaze to her, his black eyes narrowing. She stepped back, sharply aware of the current running between them.

"You bought a new cell phone, a private one, which set off a red flag."

"What I spend my money on is my business."

Tarak's lips thinned. He stepped toward her. "Are you making sure I notice you, Sabra? Ensuring your name is brought up?"

She sidestepped to avoid having to tip her head back to maintain eye contact. She didn't need to be in that position; it was too damned vulnerable. "That's majorly presumptuous. Maybe I was just following your suggestion to get a private cell phone if I wanted my conversations to be private."

He was weighing her words, his gaze cutting into hers as he tried to get at her true feelings. "Not presumptuous. I'm reading the signals your body is putting out."

"You're changing the topic."

He shrugged. "I'm adjusting to the circumstances." He took a long, leisurely look down her length and back up again. "My priorities have shifted."

She drew in a stiff breath. The way he ripped down a conversation to its base elements was raw and sexy.

"I'm not saying I don't want to jump you, but I'm making the choice not to be your fuck buddy, even though it has appeal."

He bared his teeth at her. "I woke up every damned night this week from the sounds of you coming echoing in my dreams. You're right about one thing—I want to fuck you and I'm not any closer to being able to control it than you are."

His breath was agitated by the time he finished, but her heart was accelerating to match. He took another step toward her and she lifted her chin as he reached out and stroked her neck.

It was startling, the contact between their bare skin. Her clothing felt too damned tight, and she wanted to grab his shirt and rip it wide open.

He slipped his hand around her head, gripping a handful of her hair as he pulled her against him. "I thought about kissing you all week, kissing every damned, pink part of you."

He smothered her retort beneath a hard kiss. There was no teasing, only bold conquest. He pressed her lips open and thrust his tongue deeply into her mouth. Her pussy gave a strange little contraction as she pressed up against his erection. The reasons to stay away from him crumbled as her body demanded a full taste of what she craved.

She reached for him, stretching her hand up to hold the back of his head so she could kiss him just as savagely as he was kissing her.

He stepped back, holding her at arm's length.

"Let's go," he ordered.

He grabbed her keys and had the front door open with one

rapid motion. He paused and ran a hand through his hair as he drew in a deep, raspy breath.

"Where are we—"

"Where doesn't matter as much as why." His expression tightened when he looked back at her. "If we stay here, I'm going to fuck you."

It sounded like a damned necessity to her raging need. But she worried her lower lip. "Look… I'm not sure it's a good idea to be together. You drive me a little crazy."

"You make me insane, Sabra. So step out the door before I close it and get back to letting you rip my clothes off like your eyes were telling me you wanted to do. Believe me, it's what I want."

"So why is the door open?"

"Because I don't want anyone but you. If that were the case, a week would have seen the urge dying off." He pointed at the door. "So we'll try it your way—more than just fucking. But if we stay here, you'll have to wait for the *more* part."

She wasn't really sure what he was promising her, only that she could see the strain on his face and hear it in his voice. Hell, she could feel it clawing at her insides. The word *fuck* had never been enticing before, but it was when Tarak used it—frank, blunt, but loaded with the hard promise of satisfaction.

She made it onto the porch, and he closed the door behind them, locking it before dropping the keys into his pocket.

"Control freak."

The Aston Martin beeped as he hit the remote. "I prefer 'hands on.'"

She had a feeling she was going to too.

He opened the passenger-side door and her belly did a strange flop. *Point of no return.*

Her mouth was dry but her panties were wet, so she climbed in. The scent of leather surrounded her, striking her as masculine, just like the owner. The seat cradled her and she stretched her feet out as the driver-side door opened.

Tarak pulled out of the driveway with a hard motion. He handled the beast of a car with a strength that made her bite her lip again.

She had no idea where they were going and was stunned to realize she was enjoying it. Her pride balked, but excitement was prickling along her skin.

The sun was just a glowing red orb on the horizon line. Tarak threaded his way through traffic, heading for the coast. When he exited the freeway, it was onto a more private road. It wound its way up a hillside to a private resort tucked into the bluffs overlooking the surf. He pressed the accelerator and let the car loose. It hugged the curves, taking her along for a ride that fed her growing excitement level. He had his cuffs rolled back, exposing his muscular forearms. Her attention lingered over the grip he had on the steering wheel—strong, confident, and steady.

He was in complete control. The feeling of so much raw power was almost suffocating, but she found herself on the border, balancing between excitement and feeling cornered.

The intensity was mind blowing.

The road crested, offering her a view of an Italian villa–style resort. The sides of the road were covered with colorful plants that had been expertly manicured.

The chauffeurs fought over who was going to get the keys to the Aston Martin. The faster one opened the door for Tarak, while his defeated buddy opened the passenger-side door for her.

The sea air blew her hair around. She had only a moment before Tarak was beside her, clasping her elbow and guiding her through the huge, double glass doors. The entryway was covered in marble tile with plush seating areas. Huge potted plants added a slice of nature, but it all passed in a blur.

Tarak guided her through the lobby to a set of elevators. The reception desk didn't gain even a single glance from him. He swiped a key card to open the elevator doors.

"You booked a room already?"

"A suite," he answered as the doors slid shut. "To be honest, I simply told the staff to expect me."

The elevator chimed and the doors slid open. It was a short walk to the double doors of the suite. Another flash of the key card and Tarak was pushing one side open for her.

The interior wasn't what she expected. The lobby had been done in muted tones, but the suite was decorated in rich, autumn hues. The floor was covered in clay tile with area rugs woven with Native American patterns. The vases and knickknacks were all Apache too. The main room had huge patio doors that were open to let in the sea breeze and the sound of the surf. A soft flicker danced off the polished surface of the tiles from a dozen candles lit in various places around the room.

Sabra walked toward the open doors. The entire wall of glass was sectioned and pushed back to open up the whole room. A balcony with a railing was the only thing separating her from the beach.

"You own this place," she remarked as she took another look around the suite. "This is your personal color scheme."

"It's far more cost effective than a beach house." He had his hands shoved into his pockets.

"I've never seen you nervous."

He choked on what might have been a bark of laughter. He pulled his hands loose while shaking his head. "I'm not nervous."

His tone was irrefutable—solid and every bit as hard as the man himself.

"I'm trying to act like a gentleman," he clarified. "It's proving a challenge."

It was her turn to choke. One of his dark eyebrows rose in response.

"Does that mean you prefer me… as I am?"

He was holding his true nature back. The effort itself was something that sparked a new form of respect for him inside her. It was something undefined, just a feeling of appreciation for the effort he was making.

She'd missed the table when she walked in. It was set with several dishes, steam rising in thin tapers from the sides of several chafing dishes. A bottle of wine was sitting in a polished ice bucket. He reached over, hooked the back of one of the chairs, and pulled it out for her.

That wasn't what she wanted.

In fact, she was sure sitting through a meal might just snap something inside her mind permanently.

"I like you as you are." Her tone had gone sultry. She felt more aware of her body than she could ever recall being. Her hips had taken on a life of their own, swaying with every step. She wanted to be feminine and alluring and completely captivating.

He closed the distance between them and she felt him approaching as much as she saw it. There was a raw sense of power radiating from him. It grew to a fevered pitch until he was looming over her and she had to tip her head back to lock gazes with him.

"Put your hands on me, Sabra." His eyes reflected the flicker of the candle burning on the table. "I'm going to go insane if you don't finish ripping one of my shirts off me."

She reached for him, shocked by how quickly her passion ignited. It was as if they'd never separated. Her fingers trembled but she quelled the urge to rush, needing to master the urges churning inside her. It was a desperate sort of need, one that frightened her as much as it challenged.

The first contact was jarring. A jolt of sensation pierced the restraint she'd been cultivating. All the impulses she'd been trying to corral surged forward. She reached for the open collar of his shirt and pulled it wide, popping a single button.

"Too damned slow," he snarled before taking over the task himself. He yanked on the edges of the shirt, tearing it, and sent the rest of the buttons flying. He shrugged out of the ruined garment and tossed it aside. "I want to be naked with you, Sabra."

"I know."

His chest was a feast of masculine brawn, every ridge sculpted and free of fat. She reached out and stroked him, marveling at the satin smoothness of his skin.

And the heat.

He was hot, his skin warming her fingertips and making her clothing feel suffocating.

She began pulling at her own clothing, lost in the surge of need intoxicating her senses. She kicked her shoes off and shucked her suit jacket with a shrug.

That was as far as she got before he pulled her against him.

"I'm going to strip you, Sabra."

He pressed a hot kiss against her mouth. This time, he held back and licked her lower lip before pressing her mouth open. She shivered, the need to be closer to him, entwined with him, increasing like a hunger. The rest of the world was fading away, the euphoria of the moment all she felt.

She thrust her tongue up to stroke his before he penetrated her mouth. One long, velvet stroke that drew a moan from him. A moment later, he scooped her off her feet and carried her past the table, toward the bedroom. Another section of wall was open in front of the huge bed. The sheets were deep terra-cotta, and he placed her on them like some sort of trophy. He soaked up the sight of her for a moment—one long, drawn-out bubble of time that felt like an eternity.

A moment later, he crawled over her, threading his fingers

through hers and pinning her arms to the bed. It was completely controlling but it thrilled her to the bone.

"I chickened out of sending you a note today." He angled his head and pressed a kiss against the bare skin of her throat. "I was too damned worried you'd run away."

"I might have," she admitted. "It's not as though we're in a relationship... or even should be."

He lifted his head, the flicker of the candles turning his skin a deep ruby. "To be truthful, I was worried I'd go track you down."

There was a savage glint in his eyes that made her shiver. He rubbed the back of her neck with a soothing motion. "Is that stepping over the line?"

"You step over the line just because it's there."

His lips curled and split to flash his teeth. But he pushed back, leaving the bed and making her feel abandoned.

She shook her head. Desperation was building inside her, the need threatening to suffocate her. She rolled over and reached for what she wanted, pressing her hand against the front of his pants. The feel of his rock-hard cock registered, gaining a hum of approval from every inch of her body before he stepped back, depriving her of what she craved.

"Hey..." She had to scoot to the edge of the monster-sized bed to chase him. "I thought you wanted me to put my hands on you."

"I'm more fascinated by the idea of you enjoying hearing me say I would have chased you."

She hesitated, suddenly undecided about just how close an encounter she wanted with his savage side. But she never really got past the look in his eyes. A crazy twist of excitement went through her as she hissed at him.

The sound broke through the last of his restraint. She worried her lower lip as she looked at him, undecided about just how close an encounter she wanted with his primal side, but all thinking stopped as she watched his lips curl with primitive pleasure. He lifted the loosened necktie over his head and lunged after her.

She squealed and rolled over in an attempt to flee. The bed bounced but her knees sank into the surface of it, slowing her down too much to evade him. He looped the tie around her wrist and captured her other one before she finished trying to propel herself out of his reach.

He pulled her arms above her head and knotted the tie around one of the pieces of the wrought-iron headboard.

He grabbed her top and pushed it over her head, above her elbows to bare her torso. The night breeze blew across her skin, making her shudder at the sharp contrast.

"I cursed myself for not getting a taste of your tits."

He brushed her belly, stroking upward until he cupped her breasts through her bra. The fabric was a cruel barrier, but at least she wasn't the only one who thought so. He slid his hands beneath her body and she arched up to give him room to unhook the garment. With her hands bound, he shoved it up to join her top.

"Pink nipples." He leaned down and sucked one between his lips.

Her skirt lasted a whole thirty seconds before he had it stripped off her body.

He hovered over her cleft, his breath teasing her wet slit. "I would've been willing to swear I smelled your cunt in my dreams..." He drew in a deep breath and held it. "But this is a hundred times better... more intense."

He opened his eyes and looked up her body. "You unleash something primitive in me."

She licked a suddenly dry lower lip. "The first time I saw you, I thought you should be wearing a headband, like your ancestors."

No matter how much she wanted him, she still twisted against the tie securing her to the headboard. His gaze shifted to her movements, satisfaction appearing on his face. He shrugged out of his shirt before stripping out of his slacks and tossing them aside. For just a moment, he stood there, completely bare and mouthwateringly amazing.

"As much as I want to fuck you, I want to make you come while I watch." He crawled back onto the bed and settled on his haunches, giving her a look at his cock. Her pussy craved it, need making her pull on her restraints again. His cock was… a superior package. The need to touch it overruled any notion of letting him control the moment.

"You're being a selfish pig," she accused when the silk held.

He surprised her by nodding. "I know."

There wasn't a hint of remorse in his tone. He flattened his hand on her belly and stroked his way downward, over the curves of her hips and along her thighs.

"But it's consuming me…" He reached back up and began again, this time stroking her belly and the insides of her thighs. "And you encourage me to be myself." His eyes glittered with warning. "I'm a controlling bastard."

"I'll bet," she whispered in a husky tone, a hint of uncertainty surfacing to puncture the moment.

He fingered her slit, his fingertip slipping easily between the folds of her sex because she was so aroused. She jerked when he connected with her clit, pressing down on top of the little nub with enough pressure to make her squirm. There was just no way to remain still. She needed release and her hips rose and swiveled with the urge to climax. Whatever reservations she had vaporized. It was no longer about choice. She was a slave to her needs; an addict.

"The need to control has never invaded my bedroom so completely." He watched her as he continued to finger her. "I want to know exactly how to make you groan, Sabra."

He pressed down harder, and she jerked as pleasure spiked through her. The orgasm was hard and tore through her at light speed. She bowed upward, off the surface of the bed while it wrung her, and then collapsed back down.

But opening her eyes seemed too hard. With the raging need appeased for the moment, her cheeks turned pink as she realized how much she was enjoying being dominated. It conflicted with her modern thinking to the point that she didn't want to lock gazes with Tarak.

He reached above her head and loosened her bindings. Confused, she rolled over, putting off the moment when she'd have to look at him. She felt completely exposed and vulnerable while he maintained his rock-hard exterior. He was making her into his toy, the physical pleasure surprising her with its intensity.

She'd known it would be—dreamed it, fantasized about it.

A soft crinkle drew her attention, the sound unmistakable. She turned over and watched him sheathe his huge cock with a condom in one smooth motion. Her pussy wanted a taste of his cock, but she needed something else too. She rose onto her knees, watching his gaze going to her nude breasts.

"It's my turn now."

Sabra pushed him back, crawling up to cover his body. Resistance gathered in his eyes but it died as she swung one thigh over his lean waist and settled her body over his cock.

"My turn to wring you out, Tarak."

He bared his teeth at her. "Give it your best shot."

The challenge was made, and she pressed down, gasping as his girth stretched her. But the first climax had left her slick, and her body stretched to accommodate him. It wasn't easy. His cock filled her completely, her pussy tingling as it stretched.

He cupped her hips, holding her in place for a long moment. "Easy."

She'd closed her eyes but opened them wide in response. "Like hell. I'm going to fuck you hard."

It was the coarsest thing she'd ever said, the words blunt but completely fitting her mood. She wasn't cussing; she was declaring her intent, using the words correctly for the first time in her life.

"You can try." He growled and reached for her nipples. He pinched them gently, sending her up off his cock.

"I'll succeed." She plunged down and adopted a pace that pleased the raging need threatening to consume her. He lost the battle to toy with her nipples and gripped her hips again, trying to control the pace.

"I'm fucking you, Tarak." She reached for one hand and tried to peel his fingers off her hip. His face was strained, the muscles along his neck cording as she maintained her pace. Another orgasm was already building inside her, but she resisted the urge to lean forward so her clit would gain more pressure.

She wanted to unmask him first.

He denied her that victory. With a snarl he surged up, clasping her around the waist before turning over. She yelled at him, hissing as he pinned her down.

"Asshole," she spat at him.

"Bitch," he countered as he thrust hard and deep into her.

Pleasure spiked through her. Her pussy clenched around his length, trying to milk him. He ground his hips against hers and then pounded the next few thrusts into her. It was dominating but touched some need buried beneath the carefully laid out plans she had for her life. She wanted him, wanted him to demand her. It made no sense, but it felt better than any sex she'd had in her life. It was wild, uncontrolled. When the climax burst, she moaned, the sound low and primitive. She arched, lifting her hips toward his next plunge. Her body contracted around his length and he snarled something as she felt him begin to climax. His cock was rock hard inside her, but she felt it jerking as he ejaculated.

A moment later, he collapsed on top of her, catching his weight on his elbows at the last minute. She felt his hair brushing her beaded nipples. They were puckered tight from the intensity of the orgasm.

"I'm sorry…" He offered before pushing himself back onto his haunches. It didn't feel as if she could move, so she just lay there. He studied her, a glint of satisfaction entering his black eyes.

"No, I'm not sorry, Sabra." He pushed back off the bed and tossed the used condom into the trash can. "I wanted to fuck you like that the moment I felt your garter belt strap."

He walked around the bed and scooped her up. "But I think it's time for that something more you wanted along with the mind-blowing sex."

He made his way toward the master bathroom. A giant Jacuzzi tub was bubbling gently in anticipation of their visit. Another huge, open window was set in front of it.

"I don't keep it very hot," he warned her.

He sat her on the edge of the tub and she reached in to test the temperature with her fingers. "I can understand that. You run warm."

"Apache are made by nature to survive."

He slid into the tub, settling into a portion of it that was shaped like a lounge chair. There was a pop as he stretched his back before he looked back at her. "Come here, Sabra, if you think you can handle the 'more' part."

He offered her his hand, the gesture so formal but also tender. She was reaching for it before she thought about it. Honestly, it felt as if her brain were frozen, at least when it came to any sort of deep thinking. All she wanted was to keep answering her impulses and enjoying the gratification of having them satisfied.

The water was delightful, the bubbles easing the soreness from her muscles. She settled in beside him, but he shifted and slid an arm around her waist. She wasn't sure what to make of it, stiffening out of a need to protect herself.

He sighed and pulled her all the way into his lap. His legs

separated so she was surrounded by him from head to toe. He nuzzled the top of her head, pressing a kiss onto it before settling back.

"The last time I did more with a woman, she sank a dagger into my back and sold my ring at a pawnshop."

For a long moment, the surf rolled and crashed in the distance. Sabra felt as though her emotions were mimicking their motions. Words failed her, shock holding her silent. "What a bitch," she choked out at last.

"About the same as a man who would send you a Dear Jane text message to tell you he's been cheating."

She stiffened but his arms held her in place. "You're a control freak, you know that?"

His chest vibrated with his amusement. "I like to know what is happening with the money I earned. I wasn't bragging when I said I was Nektosha. It's my child, the one I molded and breathed life into. When you pay for something, don't you expect to be able to check the details?"

"You've got a point." However, it drove home how different their lives were.

"But you're still not sure you like it?" he pressed.

Sabra drew in a deep breath. "I'm not missing the fact that you decided to match what you knew about me with your own personal information. You didn't have to tell me about your past."

He was trying, only she wasn't exactly sure of just where it was all going. He felt so good against her bare skin, part of her rebelled against thinking at all.

So she turned around and pressed a kiss against his throat. He drew in a sharp breath as she straddled him and kissed a spot beneath his jaw.

"Does this mean we're done talking?"

She sealed his lips beneath a kiss in reply. He let her lead for a moment, and she took full advantage of the opportunity. She licked his lower lip, noting the contrast between the smooth skin and the rest of his hard body.

Well, there were other smooth parts of him too.

She reached down and stroked his cock. The water made it slick, but the skin was also smooth as silk, covering a rock-hard erection that set off a renewed throbbing in her clit.

His eyes narrowed as she smoothed her hand along his length. Enjoyment tightened his features.

"It's disgusting how much you turn me on, Sabra."

"What a lovely compliment." She reached for the base again and stroked up to the crown. "It nice to know though, nice to know I'm not the only one being driven insane by this… whatever it is between us."

"Ah…" he drawled out between clenched teeth. "You've returned the compliment. I'm a… whatever."

She choked on a laugh. "Yeah, I guess I'm guilty as charged."

But she was also enjoying the moment. The need to best him was still swimming around in her head. It was an uncompleted challenge, one she wasn't in the mood to let slip away.

"On more than one account, I want to make you lose control." She curled her fingers into talons and drew them down his chest. "You won't find it so easy to flip me on my back here."

Something primitive flashed in his eyes. It complemented the flicker of candlelight and the crash of the surf. The breeze blowing in the open window was chilly but that made clinging to him even more enticing. She didn't want anything but his bare skin to warm her. He caught her hips, easing her back until she felt his cock pressing against the folds of her slit.

"Shit," he bit out, his hands tightening on her hips. "I'm not wearing a condom."

"It isn't necessary."

"Birth control pills have a failure rate." His jaw was clenched as he fought the urge to let her sheathe him. "It makes me crazy to feel your bare skin against mine, every fucking inch of it—but not at a risk."

She growled, frustration threatening to eat her alive. The impulse to just take what she wanted was there, but she wasn't going to be accused of ignoring risk factors. It was going to be an equal relationship, not something he felt he had to manage or risk opening himself up to consequences. She slapped his shoulder and used it as a balance point to stand up. The water swished as she left the Jacuzzi and ran down her body to leave a trail across the bathroom and living room floor. She heard him move in the water but didn't look behind her.

The wrapper from the first condom was sitting on the bedside table. She pulled the drawer open and found several more. Grabbing one, she turned around, marched back to the bathroom, and nearly ran into Tarak. "I've got the fucking condom. But since you're up, I've got a better idea."

The need to jump him was so intense, she was mad she wasn't already getting what she wanted.

And she was in the mood to take it.

She sank to her knees in front of him. He jerked, surprised by her abrupt motions. But she gripped his cock, pumping it several times. She looked up his magnificent body to find him watching her with hungry eyes.

"I think I'm going to enjoy this more than you are, Tarak."

And that was a first. She'd never enjoyed sucking cock particularly much. Tonight, she wanted a taste of him.

He shuddered when she licked him for the first time.

His big body rippled and she purred with delight. Closing her fingers around him, she drew her hand up to the crown before leaning forward to lick the slit on top.

"Holy Christ!"

He caught the back of her head by her hair, gathering up a fistful of it. But she didn't let him control her motions. She leaned forward and took the entire head of his cock between her lips. His skin was silky soft against her lips, the slight salty taste of his come mingling with the taste of his skin. She wanted more, so she milked the portion of his length that wasn't encased between her lips and teased the slit with the tip of her tongue.

"*Shit!*"

His voice was rough and his breathing labored. He lost his grip in her hair but renewed it as his hips thrust forward, driving more of his cock between her lips.

She wanted it to last longer, but he didn't seem to have any more control over his response to her than she did to him. He thrust a few more times before a ragged groan announced her victory. His come flooded her mouth and she sucked harder on his cock. His knees bent as pleasure ripped through him. He drew in several hard breaths as she sat back on her heels.

His face glowed with satisfaction. It was hard and basic but very much what she'd craved a glimpse of. He reached out with a hand to steady himself against the doorframe. His eyes were closed as the last of the pleasure rippled through him. It was the closest she'd ever seen him come to displaying any sort of weakness.

He opened his eyes and locked gazes with her. For just a moment, she thought she saw uncertainty in the black orbs, but they hardened as his legs straightened. He grabbed the condom off the countertop where she'd tossed it and tore the package open. One smooth motion and his cock was sheathed.

She trembled, a new rush of need moving through her so quickly, she felt dizzy. "You're an aphrodisiac."

"And you're addictive," he countered.

But her attention strayed to his cock, the soft sheen of the latex coating it fueling a desperation to have it inside her again. She should have been sated, exhausted, but the need was pulsing through her on a cellular level.

He scooped her up and carried her back to the bed. She fell back onto it without looking, completely trusting him to make sure she didn't end up on the floor.

"I could look at you like this forever."

He didn't sound as if he enjoyed that fact either. There was a note of frustration in his voice that irritated her.

But he didn't give her the chance to offer a retort. The bed rocked as he joined her, covering her completely and pinning her beneath him. It was a hard embrace but that seemed to feed a craving deep inside her. He pressed her thighs wide with his hips, opening her slit so his cock burrowed easily into her.

He set a hard pace, driving into her with deep thrusts that made her arch to take each one completely. It was rougher than any sex she'd ever had, but more satisfying too. He was pounding into her, driving his cock balls deep with every powerful motion of his hips. She heard the wet sounds of their coupling mixing with the rough sounds of their breathing and it seemed to drive her arousal up even higher. Sweat beaded on her skin, her heart working so hard it felt as if it might just burst along with the climax looming over her.

She really didn't care. All that mattered was feeding the need, appeasing the craving, and the only way to accomplish that was to meet his every thrust. In the moment of orgasm, she cried out, unable to contain everything she felt inside her body. It was as if her exterior cracked under the strain. He let out a groan, one which proclaimed victory. She opened her eyes and caught the look on his face. He bowed back, straining to bury every last bit of his cock inside her. She felt it jerk and tightened her pussy around it.

"Holy God… don't stop!"

She clenched, relaxed, and tightened her pussy again. He gasped, snarling as his body shook. For a long moment, he remained frozen before he collapsed. He rolled over, onto the bed beside her.

Her senses were filled with the scent of his sweat. It was a detail that unexpectedly pleased her right before she drifted off into oblivion.

Chapter 5

SHE SMELLED THE SUNSHINE before she opened her eyes.

The sea air just had a different scent when it was warm. Sabra rubbed her eyes and tried to wake up. Her brain took its time because she'd been in such a deep sleep. She felt absolutely wonderful though, more rested than she had in a long time.

The crash of the surf made her frown. Pushing herself up, she looked around the room. Details rushed back as she looked out onto a private stretch of beach. Down the way, she could see the sign warning beach walkers to turn back. In the distance was a couple walking, but they were too far away to see into the suite.

That was a damned good thing since she wasn't wearing a stitch.

The warm air blew over her bare skin, awakening a memory of the night before. But it was just a memory, and one she was experiencing alone too. Tarak was nowhere in sight. She swung her feet over the side of the bed and walked to the doorway to look into the other part of the suite. The untouched dinner sat on the table along with her purse. She wandered around, looking for a note, but there was nothing.

What else did I expect?

It was still bitter, but even the disappointment tearing through her fit Tarak. He always affected her in extremes.

A hot shower helped restore her balance, even if part of the reason was because it rinsed out her eyes.

No tears.

It had to be a law of the universe that anyone who spent the night with a sex demon couldn't get too caught up in the moment. She had to be practical. The man knew how to touch a woman because he practiced a whole lot.

So she needed to be nonchalant.

Modern and poised.

It sucked.

"Were you going to say good-bye?"

Sabra turned around to find Tarak coming through the doorway from the balcony. He had on a pair of jogging shorts and a towel draped around his neck. He scanned her from head to toe, taking in every detail. What bugged her was the fact that it felt like he read her expression like a book. Her attempt to be nonchalant wasn't working very well.

"You didn't bother to," she spat out before cringing at just how prissy she sounded. "I mean, yes, I was."

His eyes narrowed before he decided something and walked across the room to snag her purse off the dining table. Without a hint of regard for her privacy, he yanked the zipper open and searched the contents.

"I sent you a text." He tossed her cell phone at her. "I guess I should have thought about writing a note."

She caught the phone and saw the new text message waiting for her. "How did you get my new number?"

"You signed an agreement to submit to random security checks." He wiped his forehead with the towel before finishing. "I told you last night your new number put up a red flag. Security gave me the number within hours of you signing the contract with the carrier."

"So much for a private line being private."

He shrugged, unrepentant. "You want to work on the sixteenth floor? Deal with the Defense Department's demands."

"Somehow, I think this is about your demands."

He walked into the kitchen and grabbed a glass from a cabinet. He flipped on the faucet and filled it with water. When it was full, he turned around and leaned against the counter.

"I wanted to know if you went back to Kevin." He drew a long sip of water. "I couldn't keep my mind off you for even a single day. It was burning a hole in my mind, thinking you were using him to satisfy the passion you had for me."

He set the water down with a sharp motion. A moment later, he had her pulled up against his body. Even his sweat smelled good.

"I want you to stay, Sabra."

It was a strange combination of order and plea. He rubbed her nape, trying to soothe her into compliance.

She shuddered. Her body responded to his instantly. She flattened her hands against his chest but lost the urge to push him away the moment she felt the hard muscles. Her lips went dry as she realized just how fast she was succumbing to him again.

She drew in a deep breath to steady herself. "Maybe it's healthy for us to take a few hours off…"

"That's what I thought when I went running."

He stroked her back, moving one hand down to cup her bottom and press her forward. His cock was rigid beneath the soft jersey of his shorts.

"It didn't work out as planned."

A wave of heat moved slowly through her belly. It was tempting, so enticing, but it felt as if a warning bell was going off at the same time, telling her she was on a path that was going to lead her straight into obsession.

"This is freaking me out a little," she confessed. "The sex is great but—"

"Leaving at first light makes you the one who wants no strings attached." He sounded irritated, which grated on her nerves. She pushed against his chest. His grip tightened on her nape before he released her.

"Don't you want more?" she asked.

He grabbed the water glass and drained it.

"Don't you want something beyond sex?" she pressed.

He was looking at the empty glass on the marble kitchen countertop. He was avoiding her stare, concealing his true feelings. It hurt more than waking up alone had.

"Okay, well I guess if you just want to be a tool in the bedroom. That's your business."

He laughed, the sound low and menacing. With a sharp motion, he turned around and faced her. Tarak crossed his arms over his chest and leveled a scathing look at her.

"It's nothing but a bullshit game." His tone was razor-sharp. "A primitive holdover that's sunk so far into your brain, you don't even realize the reason you want a relationship is because you need to trust me enough to let me get on top of you. It's a survival instinct, nothing more."

She wanted to get mad. It should have been easy since he was taking callousness to a new level. But her memory refused to let her forget what he'd confessed. He had feelings, somewhere under all the walls he'd built up.

"She really tore a hole in you."

His eyebrows lowered defensively. "Who?"

"The one who sold your ring at a pawnshop." His complexion darkened, but she didn't let him have enough time to form a retort. "I'm leaving because I'm not interested in sharing you with her ghost. Call me if you decide to get past that breakup."

She grabbed her purse and her heels tapped against the title as she made her way to the door.

Pain was tearing up the memories of the last twenty-four hours as she opened the door and stepped out into the elevator lobby.

It was as though a beast were trying to destroy every last golden moment she thought she'd experienced.

She was too agitated to wait for the elevator so she opted for the stairs. Moving kept her busy, too busy to let her emotions seep through the cracks in her composure.

Sex demons sucked at morning afters.

—⁓—

Tarak had marked her.

Sabra lifted her hand and studied the pink marks around her wrist on the way home. A faint twist of excitement went through her belly.

All right, she'd been an accessory to the crime.

She leaned her head back and tried to clear her mind. It wasn't going to be easy, but once again she reminded herself that she'd known how giving in to her hunger for Tarak was going to end.

Her car was still sitting in the driveway when the cab pulled up at the curb. She peered into the front seat to read the meter.

The driver was already out and on his way around to open her door. She fumbled with some bills and offered them to him as she stood up.

"No, ma'am. Mr. Nektosha has an account with us."

Of course he did. A fuck pad needed a morning-after cleanup crew after all.

She handed the guy a five and rummaged around inside her purse for her house keys. It was a beautiful early spring day, the California sky blue and clear. But all she wanted to do was get inside and hide.

Some modern, poised woman she was turning out to be.

—⁓—

He went to his beach suite for privacy. That was its purpose in his life.

Tarak stepped into the shower and let the cold water slap him back into normalcy.

It didn't work as well as planned. The moment he crossed into the bedroom, he spied the tangled sheets and his tie still hanging from the headboard.

She didn't want to share him with a ghost?

Of course not. No woman wanted to share.

But the silence shamed him with just how easily she'd walked away from him. No pleading look. No attempt to wring a promise of a call from him, just a determined look in her eyes as she stuck to what she felt was important. His money had always been enough to get other women to adjust their rules to suit his decisions.

Not Sabra.

She was just gone, and for the first time in a very long time, he discovered himself missing the company he'd so easily discarded.

But he had no idea what it meant.

"Don't think you are canceling brunch." Celeste clicked her tongue on the other end of the phone line. "I have been saving up my calories all weekend, so you'd better be getting ready."

"I'm not very good company," Sabra admitted, ashamed at how she'd let the better part of Saturday drift into nothingness. Sunday morning wasn't looking any more promising either.

"Well, I am excellent company," Celeste purred. "I'll be in your driveway in twenty-two minutes. Choose the setting for your interrogation."

There was a soft, evil-sounding cackle on the other end of the line before it cut off. Sabra couldn't help but smile. Celeste was a master at worming details out of people, and she enjoyed it.

And hiding from the world wasn't the answer, so when Celeste pulled her Corvette into the driveway, Sabra was ready for her. At least she hoped she was.

Celeste drove into the city before heading up a hill. The restaurant she pulled up in front of had a view of the entire valley. The champagne brunch was in full swing as they walked through the atrium toward the front doors. Water tinkled in a fountain as the scent of jasmine filled the morning air. Two doormen opened the double doors for them as the maître d' offered them a smile. The moment they sat down, Celeste fluttered her eyelashes and ordered something from the kitchen. As usual, the staff was falling over themselves to serve her unfairly attractive sidekick. Iced tea arrived right on the heels of their order being taken.

"You always want to have brunch, but you never take anything off the buffet."

Celeste gave a delicate shrug. "I'm a germophobe."

"You know the waiter is just dishing up what is waiting in the warming pans," Sabra predicted.

Celeste winkled her nose. "I bet you there will be steam rising from the plate he delivers; lots of steam to prove the cook made me something fresh. So why was your car in the driveway Friday night?"

The interrogation was commencing. A gleam of anticipation entered Celeste's green eyes as she pegged Sabra with a knowing glance. "I was there at seven sharp for our girls' night out."

"Oh crap." Sabra reached for her iced tea and took a sip. "I'm sorry. I completely forgot."

"You didn't check your text messages either," she continued. "I was very put out. Went home and spent the night surfing Facebook posts in search of companionship."

Sabra snorted. "Oh right."

A waiter appeared with a plate that was indeed steaming. He placed it in front of Celeste with a practiced flourish. He sat another plate down in front of Sabra before retreating.

"Admit it," Celeste insisted as she used the side of her fork to cut into her omelet. "You got over your trust issues with Tarak Nektosha."

"Well, I wouldn't go that far. We've still got plenty of trust issues. Actually, I'm not sure we have anything at all anymore."

Celeste froze with her fork in the air on the way to her mouth. Her green eyes were fixed on Sabra's wrist where the faint pink marks were.

"You let him tie you up?" Her friend was furious. Rage made her tremble.

"It was just a spontaneous thing," Sabra muttered, but she cringed when she felt her cheeks turning red. Celeste didn't miss it either.

"That's how it starts." Her eyes widened with knowledge that was painful for her. "And then they have to keep topping their last high, like a junkie. Never satisfied with what they had the last time. Don't let him treat you like that. He's just a selfish pig who thinks the world is his toy store."

"It's nothing to get so worked up over. It's over."

Celeste warned, her eyes still glowing with rage. "I hope so, Sabra. He's a dangerous man, one with enough money to make most complications with the law disappear. Don't trust his kind. They play by different rules."

"I know."

But that didn't stop Sabra from thinking about him for the rest of the day. Sunday afternoon stretched on for what felt like an eternity. It tormented her with thoughts of what she'd find waiting for her on Monday morning. The only relief she found was by sitting down at her computer and taking a look at the want ads. But there was no way any major company was going to overlook the seven-month blip on her résumé. A short tenure like that was going to set off alarm bells. Sure, Tarak had been completely professional, but Celeste was right, he was used to controlling his world. If he wanted her out of it, she'd be gone.

She marked several possible positions and updated her work history before turning in for the night.

She'd deal with whatever came. It was the Donovan way.

"Another, Mr. Nektosha?"

Tarak nodded and the flight attendant looked surprised. But she masked it quickly, plastering a smile on her lips and returning to the private jet's galley. He cussed softly when she delivered the whisky. The last woman who'd driven him to excess was Liluye.

But he liked drinking to Sabra's memory better.

That fact made him put the tumbler down. Sabra wasn't lost to him unless he let her slip through his fingers. The jet engines droned on in the background as they propelled him north toward Alaska.

He was running away.

It was the honest truth, and it made him take a step back to think about his actions. A coward would spend his entire life running and never understand his own soul. His grandfather had told him that more times than he could count, enough so that the words rose inside his head in the same crusty voice the old man had near the end of his days.

A warrior did not run; he looked on his own nature and found peace in understanding himself.

His nature was always at odds with the modern world, but he'd be lying if he didn't admit to enjoying the struggle. He thrived on adrenaline.

He turned his chair and faced his laptop. Drinking wasn't the answer; action was.

It was time to put the ball back in Sabra's court.

Monday faded away too easily for how much she'd worried about it. Nothing on the sixteenth floor was different. Her inbox was brimming and the project meetings still progressed at a speedy clip. Security didn't show up to escort her to the pavement. More of the other VPs relaxed around her too.

No matter what else she thought about Tarak, she had to admire him for keeping their personal relationship out of the office. Her respect grew for him by a huge amount.

Of course, that was helped along by the fact that he was nowhere to be seen. It was comforting in a way, but unnerving too. She found herself waiting for him to surface as the week progressed.

Right. He's done with you, sugar. Fucked you right out of his system.

Billionaires didn't tend to give women who had walked out on them much of their time. At least that was what she'd heard.

Celeste would be happy.

Sabra's martial arts training took care of her sleeplessness by completely exhausting her. She'd never realized her butt could hurt so much after just an hour of working out. The meager supply of over-the-counter painkillers she kept in her bathroom cabinet was running low by the end of the week.

When Friday rolled around, she found herself relaxing completely. The opportunity to celebrate another week in her new position was welcome. At five o'clock on the dot, Claudia knocked on the door.

"Have a nice weekend, Claudia."

Her secretary didn't stand in the doorway as she normally did when bidding Sabra good night. Instead, she walked across the office and laid a thick overnight-express business-sized envelope on the desk.

"Mr. Nektosha asked that this be delivered to you at the close of business today."

There was a formal tone in Claudia's voice, one which made Sabra's stomach knot.

"Thank you," she managed before her secretary turned and escaped.

Sabra stared at the envelope, her hands frozen. It took a moment for her brain to thaw out enough for her to reach for the thing. It was dirty from traveling through the mail system. She pulled the strip to open it and took a deep breath to steel herself against what she was going to find inside.

She began to tear open the top. The sound of ripping paper seemed too loud.

Her phone rang, making her jump. She grabbed it and fumbled it because she was so nervous. It slid across her desk, and she slammed her knee as she lunged after it. Pain coursed through her as she turned the touch screen over so she could read the caller ID.

She didn't recognize the number but slid her fingertip across the screen to answer it anyway. A distraction was a distraction and she was desperate.

"Hello?"

"Did Claudia deliver the package?"

Tarak's voice sent a shiver down her back. The previous week evaporated. It felt as though he'd materialized from her fantasies.

"Um… yes. She did."

"I have decided to give you a counter offer, Ms. Donovan," he informed her in a hard tone.

"A what?" She dumped the contents of the package onto her desk. A printout of an airline itinerary and a bank ledger stared back at her.

"A counter offer," he confirmed. "You said you weren't interested in sharing me with Liluye. I'm proposing you join me, and we see how well you can do at making sure I have no time to dwell on my past."

Her heart leapt at the thought of seeing him again. Excitement bubbled through her, threatening to make her giddy. She forced herself to swallow it and try and maintain her composure. "I'm not sure that's a good idea."

"Because I'm your boss?"

"That's one good reason. But I'm a little more stuck on the explosive chemistry between us."

"I've been stuck on it too." There was a low, male sound of frustration on the other side of the line. "I've decided it's time for action."

She closed her eyes, sealing her lips to keep him from hearing the little gasp of delight that rose from her in response.

"There's two hundred grand deposited in that bank account. It's yours as a backup plan."

She swiped the bank ledger and opened it. "A what?" It didn't seem possible to be holding the key to two hundred thousand dollars in her hands.

"A security measure—one which will override your argument of not mixing pleasure with business. The fact that I am your boss is nullified."

"People are going to notice—"

"I am offering you a position in our Alaskan office, located on the design and development grounds. Your property will be maintained while you are out of the state. There is also a ticket for the ten o'clock flight for Anchorage. That's enough money to see you through until you find another company to work for if you don't want to stay at Nektosha if our personal relationship fails. There's a letter from my lawyer as well, signed, sealed, and ready to hold up in any court against the threat of me trying to come after the money. Log in and transfer the funds before you leave. There is also a return ticket, good anytime."

"That's... um—" Her mind went blank.

"A brilliant maneuver on my part," he said, cutting her off. "I've removed any possible argument you can make against a relationship with me based on needing your income."

She tried to think of an argument but the only one was to admit that she was too chicken to see what would happen if they spent more time together.

"Okay, it is brilliant. I'll give you that."

It was also intimidating. Tarak lived in a vastly different world than she did.

Her cheeks were heating up, but she wasn't sure if it was the idea of seeing him or annoyance with his ability to cut off her avenues of escape. It was boiling down to an issue of courage and if she had the guts to face him again. "Did you say Anchorage?"

"Yes. I'm at one of our testing tracks. I bought you an airline ticket instead of sending my jet for you to minimize the paper trail."

"So it's between you and me."

"Exactly."

It was ruthless, so in line with the way he'd struck her the first time they met. There was something else though, something more, and that was what made her check the airline itinerary closer for details. A tingle went through her as she pondered the idea that she was important enough for him to want her to not have any objections.

"You suck at issuing invitations," she decided. "This is more like a battlefield plan."

He snorted. "Are you coming, Sabra?" His question was guarded, but it was a question.

"Possibly."

There was a pause on the other end of the line. "Why the hesitation?"

"What sort of VP would I make if I made snap decisions?" she purred softly. "It's important to check the details."

He chuckled menacingly. "You're coming."

"Really? So sure about that?"

"Positive," he bit out. "I can hear the heat in your voice, Sabra. The challenge is exciting you. I bet your nipples are hard with anticipation. I know my cock is."

The line went dead, but she was busy looking down her body. Two little bumps marked where her nipples were poking at her blouse. They tingled behind the cups of her bra, the delicate skin eager for another encounter with Tarak.

It was the perfect setup. She looked at the bank book and logged into the website. Once she tapped in the account number and the security codes in the little book, the website gave her complete access to the money. She stared at the number for a long time, just trying to soak up what it meant.

What it was, was a challenge.

A hard, impossible to ignore challenge.

She hesitated with her fingers poised over the keyboard for a long moment. Her pride didn't want to let her take the money. But her logic just couldn't quite make a valid argument against it. Tarak was right; he'd removed a significant obstacle. She typed in her account numbers and watched as the transfer went through. The system gave her a transaction number that she stared at for a full minute because it just seemed too simple for such an amount of money.

In Tarak's world, it wasn't all that much, but it was a huge gesture from a man who had told her emotions were just a hold-over from evolution. The problem with it was that now he was once again something she could have. Straight sex, even with a sex demon, wasn't enough for her. His hard line on emotions not being needed had enabled her to begin separating her need for him from her feelings.

Now they rushed back in. Her clit was throbbing softly, the sound of his voice echoing in her ear.

There was a knock on her door. She looked up to see the floor security chief standing there. Mr. Kim was as neat and sharp looking as always in a black suit. He stepped inside once she'd made eye contact with him. There was a soft rattle as a man pushed a rolling cart inside.

"Your personal things will be boxed and shipped to your new office, Ms. Donovan."

Her personal phone buzzed as a text message came in.

Don't bother to pack, your needs have been seen to.

She shook her head and typed in a reply.

All right, Tarak. You win this round.

She stood up and collected her purse. The security chief held out his hand as she neared him and pointed at her badge. It took only a little tug to remove it, but she felt the parting a lot deeper. The walk to the elevator seemed long, but at least the ride down to the ground was quick. Sabra stepped into the parking garage but stopped when she found Deanna waiting for her.

"I'll turn your keys over to the property management team." She held out her hand for the car keys dangling from Sabra's grip. "Mr. Nektosha has provided a car to get you to the airport."

Parked next to her little, practical car was a sleek, dark-windowed sedan. A man in a suit stood next to the passenger door, a hat on his head and dark shades hiding his eyes.

Deanna came closer, cupping her hand beneath the keys so all Sabra had to do was release her grip on them.

"They've needed a top-of-the-line analyst up there for a long time."

Sabra looked away from the private car and locked gazes with Deanna.

"They're lucky to have you joining them."

Sabra let go of her keys, and her former boss gave her a sharp nod.

"Really lucky." Deanna repeated. "Good luck."

The driver opened the door, proving he was tuned in to everything she was doing. It was exciting and terrifying. The two emotions flooding her with equal intensity as she slid into the back of the car. It really was a different world, one that looked inviting with all its personal service. At least until you realized your personal privacy was being sacrificed in order for those amenities to be in place.

A few moments after the door closed, the driver pulled out. But her phone vibrated with another text message, proving Deanna had dutifully informed her boss of Sabra's progress.

I can't wait to take care of you myself, Sabra.

Chapter 6

THE TICKET WAS FOR first class. Sabra sat back and marveled at the meal the steward offered her. Getting to the airport had been a frantic fight against Friday-night traffic, and she'd insisted on going home first, which put them further behind. There was just something too submissive about leaving town with nothing but the clothes on her back.

Hell, there were a lot of things about her relationship with Tarak that were too submissive. He lived in a different world than she did.

But he wasn't any happier.

That thought stuck in her head. Her dad had been fond of telling her money didn't solve all a man's troubles. He still had to look himself in the eye every morning. It couldn't ensure health, and it couldn't buy love.

At least not hers.

Sure about that?

She didn't care for the doubt surfacing inside her. The roomy first-class seat made it hard to ignore, though. The two hundred grand sitting in her savings account was another. Being free from the normal worries was welcome indeed.

It left her trying to decide what there was between Tarak and herself. She drifted off into sleep as she pondered it.

—⁓—

"You're where?" Celeste wasn't happy. "I can't believe you're flying up to Alaska to see him. Are you insane? They have, like, two state troopers per village up there. Calling 911 isn't going to bring you the same sort of response."

"I think Anchorage is a little more civilized," Sabra countered.

"Don't bet on it," Celeste snapped. "It's called the last great frontier for a reason. There's going to be tons of snow still on the ground. Didn't the design team get delayed by a blizzard? Did you go to the airport straight from the office?"

"Ah… yes, but I don't really have anything for Alaska." Sabra looked down at her leather heels. Halfway to her destination, she was catching a connecting flight and her toes were already cold. A clothing store near the gate caught her eye. "I think I'm going to do a little shopping before they call boarding."

"I doubt they have snow boots in a terminal."

"I know." Sabra walked toward the shop, eyeing the yoga pants on display. "And I know you're worried about me. I don't know what to say, but I feel as if I have to do this."

Celeste was quiet on the other end of the line. "Just keep your guard up. Don't be impressed with his tactics. Money doesn't mean as much to him as it does you and me. Neither will your heart."

She wanted to argue but couldn't find any hard facts to use. All she had were feelings. They were flooding her and making it impossible to think rationally. She'd be a liar if she didn't admit she liked the giddy sensation of knowing Tarak had taken the time to plan how to get her near him again.

Or that the idea of being alone with Tarak wasn't worth every risk she was about to take.

—◦◦◦—

Anchorage wasn't as remote as Celeste had implied. When the plane touched down, there were several gates along the terminal servicing other aircraft.

But it was covered in snow. Sabra pressed her face into the small window opening to get a look at the white stuff. The Californian in her shivered.

It was pushed off to the sides of the runways but blew around like white sand. The yoga outfit that had kept her cozy for the flight felt skimpy as the plane pulled into the gate. The steward was busy handing thick coats to the other passengers in first class, but Sabra hadn't brought one along. Back in the economy cabin, people were pulling zippers up and putting hats on. A few odd looks were cast her way as the door was opened and everyone began to file off.

The moment she stepped into the Jetway, the cold hit her. She sucked in her breath and tried to walk faster, but two people in front of her were taking their time getting to the terminal, their thick coats making it a comfortable walk for them.

By the time she made it inside again, she was hopping around trying to keep warm. Her phone buzzed and she pulled it out of her purse.

"Welcome to Anchorage."

"A damn chilly welcome," she groused. "You could have warned me there was still snow."

There was a suspicious choking sound on the other end of the line. "I thought you were a competent manager who would be proving her worth by double-checking the details."

"It would serve you right if I decided to use that return ticket now."

"I'd have to buy the seat next to you, and it would be a very long flight considering how we affect each other; no privacy for twelve hours."

Her cheeks heated as she made her way through the secured section of the terminal. She tucked her phone back into her purse and tried to steady her nerves. Men wearing hunting suits mingled with the business passengers. There was a rustic edge to their features and a practical look to them. They wore heavy boots, and sturdy clothing covered them. She passed by a huge stuffed bear inside a glass display case, its teeth over an inch long.

The chill made her pass by quickly, walking through the security checkpoint. She spotted Tarak instantly. Her gaze was drawn to his. It was like a magnetic pull. Her lower lip went dry as a shiver went down her back that had nothing to do with the chill.

He had black boots on and black snow pants. A matching jacket was open to reveal a fitted athletic thermal top. His lips curled in greeting.

But she wasn't sure how to proceed. Her mind went blank, her thoughts freezing and leaving her floundering in front of the man who consumed her.

Tarak didn't appear to be any more sure than she of what to do. He stood for a long time, just studying her. His black eyes glittered with satisfaction, sending a rush of heat through her. He wanted her, and part of her latched on to that knowledge with a grip which stunned her. Arousal snaked through her and it didn't build this time but burst into full flame. She felt like she was going into heat.

"This isn't what I want to do," he spoke at last.

His words cut through the giddy sensation she'd been enjoying since leaving southern California. "What are you talking about?"

"This." He reached down and pulled a bag off the polished tile floor. "I'd enjoy it far more if I were telling you to take your clothing off."

Two men walking nearby turned and smirked at them. They looked her up and down before flipping Tarak a thumbs-up.

He cupped her elbow and guided her toward a restroom sign. "Welcome to Alaska. Population male."

She reached for the bag, but he pulled her against him and kissed her. It was as if she'd forgotten how good his kisses were. She was suddenly desperate for it. He cupped her face and slid his lips across hers before boldly penetrating her mouth with his tongue. He thrust it deep, seeking hers and stroking it with a long lap.

A cheer went up from behind them. He pulled back, allowing

her to look at the two men who'd been watching them hoot with enjoyment. Tarak thrust his hands into his jacket pockets.

"Go on, before I follow you in there and risk security having to haul us out with our pants down."

"As blunt as always."

His lips thinned in response. "Exactly the way you like it."

She shivered and dove around the corner before she replied. Replying was a bad idea; it would only lead one place—a bathroom stall—and she was pretty sure she wouldn't be able to keep her mouth sealed while he fucked her. She certainly hadn't been able to before.

The snow pants came all the way over her waist. There was even a bib front that did nothing for her figure. But they did wonders for cutting the chill. He'd brought her the thickest pair of socks she'd ever seen, but they were soft and squishy once she pushed her feet into the boots the bag yielded. A jacket completed the outfit, and she sighed as she warmed up.

A price tag was still dangling from one cuff and she snapped it off. The amount made her cringe. Celeste's warning replayed in her mind, but it wasn't enough to keep her from walking back out to meet Tarak. No matter what happened, she needed to face it—because she was more afraid of spending the rest of her life wondering what might have been.

———

Their ride met them at the curb. The Nektosha all-terrain vehicle rolled up to stop in front of them with a crunch of snow beneath its huge tires.

"Nice," Sabra remarked when Tarak opened the door for her.

"Glad you approve. This is a test model."

The all-terrain vehicle was called a Terrain Tank. It had tires that came up to her shoulders. Each one was crafted with huge grooves to make sure it got lots of traction in deep snow. There was a step attached to the side for ease in getting into it.

"I guess there is no better place to test a snow vehicle than Alaska."

Inside there were comfortable seats, but each one had a five-point harness in place of seat belts. She pulled one over her head and snapped it into the metal bracket that sat in front of her chest. A driver sat behind the wheel. He pulled smoothly into traffic the moment Tarak closed the passenger-side door. The dashboard was alive with displays.

"It's ten below?"

"Sure is." Tarak winked at her. "Really warming up."

"Ha ha."

"What we got here, boss?" the driver inquired with a jovial tone. "It's a little early for the snow birds to be returning."

"It's not too early for this one," Tarak insisted.

There was an ease to the conversation that surprised her. Until she realized that the testing facility was where Tarak created his designs. It was his workshop and a part of his personality no one really had a clue to. The way the driver chuckled suggested far more camaraderie than she'd ever suspected Tarak of.

It gave her a spark of hope for something deeper between them as well.

The driver headed out of the city and finally turned into a driveway which had a security gate. He reached up and pressed a remote clipped to the sun visor. The gate began to slide open a moment later.

"This is Nektosha's development and Arctic testing division."

She soaked up the details as they drove across what looked like a cross between an airfield and a racetrack. There were hangars all over the place, their roofs sloped to let the snow slip off. The white stuff built up in heaps next to the buildings. In the distance, someone was actually riding a sled pulled by a team of dogs.

The driver headed toward a huge log cabin–style house. It had several different sections but it was constructed of massive logs. He pulled up and Tarak was out of the passenger seat in a flash.

He pulled open her door as she fussed with the seat restraint and finally got it open.

"That's an interesting note. The latch is too stiff for a woman."

He was making an honest observation, but it was slightly unnerving too. This was his world and a harsh one at that. She wanted to be able to rise to the challenge.

The house was magnificent.

Once inside, she sighed as warm air hit her frozen nose. The doors opened into an entryway that had benches and hooks on the wall for their coats. There was another set of doors which would let them into the house. She shrugged out of her coat and sat down to remove her boots. Nonslip carpets lined the floor, chunks of dirty snow already scattered on top of them.

"Okay?"

She looked up to find Tarak watching her. She caught just a hint of indecision in his eyes before he turned and took a lighter-weight jacket off a hook near the interior doors and offered it to her.

"Yeah, I think so." She stood but kept her attention on the jacket. He cupped her chin and raised it so their gazes locked again.

"You're not," he decided in a hard tone.

"That's the same tone you use in the boardroom." Her temper had flash lit. "I'm not here to see my boss."

His eyes narrowed, and his lips curled back menacingly. He didn't give her much time to study his response before he dropped the inside jacket and clasped her wrist tightly. He jerked her toward him with a sharp motion. She bumped into him and felt his breath against her ear.

"I'm still going to tell you exactly what I want from you," he promised.

She shivered with growing excitement. "If you're a good boy, I might even give it to you, Tarak."

He grasped her hips, the hold sending a jolt of need through her. His chest vibrated with a low sound of male appreciation. "You might be the only woman alive I'd consider trying to behave for."

Her hand was resting on his waist. She smoothed a path across his flat, toned belly before boldly clasping his cock. "That would be disappointing. You strike me as a man who makes his own rules." She raised her head so she could look into his eyes. "You make me eager to misbehave."

"Thank God." He cupped the side of her face and sealed her lips beneath his. It was the balm she needed for the week of second-guessing. She stretched up onto her toes, seeking what she'd craved since walking out on him.

He tasted better than she recalled. He was hard and unpredictable, but that satisfied her like nothing ever had before. But he pulled back and held on to her hair to keep her from following him.

"I'm dangerously close to fucking you up against the wall. I swore I wouldn't do that."

He drew in a harsh breath before reaching down and grasping her wrist again. She got only a glimpse of the interior of the house before he was pulling her behind him, up toward a set of double doors. The fact that he was taking her away to fuck her made her crazy with excitement. It licked at her insides like some kind of beast. The man affected her so intensely.

He pushed open a door and tugged her through the doorway and toward the bed. For a moment he paused and stood between her and the doorway. His black eyes glittered with satisfaction, making her breath catch.

"I don't think I would mind."

He pulled his shirt over his head, baring the sculpted perfection of his chest. "You're encouraging me, Sabra."

She shrugged and reached for the hem of her top. "Is that a problem, or are you doubting my sincerity?"

He opened the button fly of his jeans, allowing his cock freedom. The swollen organ fell right through the separated front.

God, she wanted a taste of it.

"I doubt my ability to control myself." He pushed the jeans down his legs and kicked them aside. "You unleash something inside me. All I think about is fucking."

It wasn't a traditional compliment, but it struck her as being more sincere than any praise she'd ever received from a man.

"Why do you think I got on that plane?" She pulled her top up and over her head. It fluttered to the floor behind her as she reached back to unhook her bra and bare her breasts for him. "I have the same problem. Where are the condoms?"

His eyes narrowed, becoming slits as she stripped her pants and underwear off. He was soaking up the sight of her, scrutinizing every last inch of her body. The sheer magnificence of his body put her on edge, and her confidence crumbled. She shifted, crossing one foot in front of the other and shielding her chest with her hands.

He shook his head slowly. "Don't hide from me, Sabra. You've turned me into a mindless animal. All I can think about is getting between your legs. Doubt my control or motives, but never doubt your allure. It's off the scale."

He closed the distance between them, and her heart accelerated with every step. She would have sworn she felt his body heat reaching out to entice her. He cupped her hips, the touch too gentle for what she craved.

"That works for me."

His grip tightened as his nostrils flared.

"The mindless thing." Her lower lip had gone dry, so she licked it. "It sounds really… enticing."

He growled at her, the sound turning up the arousal burning

inside her. She had no idea what she was doing, only that she couldn't regret a single thing.

He turned her around and she fell forward onto the huge bed. She flattened her hands on the surface as he leaned over her back, the hard muscles of his chest delighting her when they pressed against her.

"Sure about that, Sabra?" His voice was rough with need. He nipped the side of her neck, sending a jolt of pleasure straight into her pussy. "Sure you want to let me off the leash?"

The head of his cock slipped between the folds of her slit. It settled against the opening of her body, tormenting her with how close he was to filling her.

"I never asked you to wear a leash, and the condom was your issue."

"I don't want to wear one."

He thrust into her, his cock stretching her once again. She moaned, low and deep as pleasure threatened to explode inside her from that single stroke.

But she wanted more. Much more.

So did he.

A dressing mirror sat across the room. When she opened her eyes, she stared straight into the reflection of the two of them. He was watching her with his teeth bared.

"Don't you dare come yet."

He grasped her hips and began to pump his cock in and out of her. He leaned back and growled. "Watching your tits jiggle is so damned hot."

She couldn't seem to keep her eyes open. It was as if all the need inside her was too much to deal with, so her other senses were shutting down. She pressed her bottom back to meet each thrust, her clit throbbing with the need to climax.

It remained maddeningly out of reach. She was on the edge,

each thrust the one she thought would end her torment. His cock felt harder and bigger every time he sent it back into her too. Her lips curled back as she snarled with need.

"Satisfy me!"

He swore, but she was so far gone the words failed to register beyond being profane. He lifted her up by her hips and pushed her further onto the bed. She tried to turn over, to give her clit the pressure it craved, but he followed her and pinned her down before she could flip over.

"No!"

"Yes!" he growled next to her ear.

The bedding had bunched up and her belly rested on a mound of it. He thrust back into her, hard and deep from behind once again. This time he covered her back and pinned her down with his larger body, even tucking his chin against the side of her neck.

"And yes, I will satisfy you." He reached beneath her hips and found her clit. "But my way, Sabra. *Mine.*"

He bit her, his teeth nipping the delicate skin of her neck as he fingered her clit. The two sensations ripped through her and collided. The force of the collision sent an orgasm roaring through her. If she hadn't been lying on the bed, she was sure she would have collapsed. There was nothing but the mind-numbing pleasure, nothing but the overwhelming sensation of delight tearing through her. She screamed, the sound echoing around the room, and he snarled next to her ear as she felt him begin to come inside her. The first spurts were thick and hot against her insides. But her pussy tightened, pulling on his length as a second climax gripped her.

"That's it... milk me."

He sounded agonized, but a look in the mirror showed her an expression of primitive enjoyment. It was hard and basic, the muscles along his neck corded and as stiff as his cock.

His cock jerked a few final times before he rolled over and

collapsed on his back. The bed was huge, leaving plenty of room for them both to lay sprawled out on it.

The only sound in the room was their labored breathing. There was a slight buzzing in her ears and she felt as if she were spinning around in a lazy circle. Maybe she was going to pass out. It really didn't worry her too much. Satisfaction was glowing inside her, making every muscle lax.

Burning wood popped in the fireplace, and she opened her eyes as reality came flooding back in, keeping her from relaxing. She rolled over and got to her feet. Tarak was asleep.

She stared for a long moment at his relaxed face. A shudder moved down her back because even in sleep, the man wasn't anywhere near having his guard down. It was just too much a facet of his personality. Yet it felt like a privilege to view him in such a relaxed state. It was intimate in a manner she'd never applied the word to before. He wasn't a man who let his guard down often or even when others might witness it.

She grabbed her pants and top, and got into them without bothering with her underwear. The cabin-style home had wood flooring that was colder the closer to the entryway she went.

There was a huge great room which stretched between the double doorway of the master bedroom and the kitchen. On the right side of the kitchen there was another large room with sofas and recliners. A large fireplace was set into one wall, and the exterior wall was set with enormous picture windows. The view was amazing. A hallway led back to what was likely more bedrooms, but the master bedroom was separated for privacy and proximity to the kitchen.

She stopped, staring at her bag. It was sitting inside the entry doors of the coatroom with her purse sitting neatly on top.

Her cheeks colored as she realized she'd never taken them out of the Terrain Tank. The driver must have brought her things in after she and Tarak retired to the bedroom.

Retired to the bedroom?

Hell. They'd been in a hurry to get naked. And there was no polite way to phrase it.

Not that she was searching for one. To be completely honest with herself, she had to face the fact that she liked Tarak with all his sharp edges. She sat her bag down on the table quietly and opened it. The last thing she'd packed was her garter belt.

Nope, she didn't want him to change one little bit. Celeste would likely have something to say about her conforming to Tarak's tastes. But even that wasn't enough of a deterrent. Maybe it was the week she'd just spent thinking about Tarak, who had left her, willing to see if there was anything else to their attraction beyond fucking.

Maybe it was the fact that he'd taken the time to remove the obstacles between them. One look at the rest of the cabin, and it was clear two hundred grand wasn't much in his world. What mattered was the thought he'd invested in making sure she wouldn't have a valid argument left against continuing their relationship—it was show up or admit he was just too much for her.

"I told you not to pack anything."

Even sprawled out buck naked, the man sounded commanding. She looked back over her shoulder at him. He was frowning at her bag like it was some sort of breach of contract. Celeste's warning gained a little volume, but all it served to do was make her want to poke him a few times to see how he reacted.

"I guess I'll just forget about wearing the garter belt for you." She turned her tone sweet as honey and lifted the satin creation up so he could see it. "What was I thinking?" She dropped it back into the bag and pulled the zipper shut.

He sat up, his eyes narrowing.

"Oh yes, I was thinking I wasn't your sex kitten. Because if that's what you want, obedience to every little instruction no matter how asinine, you called the wrong girl. You're not the only one who likes things the way they like it. I brought my makeup, my personal things because I know what I like, and if you know what brand of bra I'm wearing, you're going to qualify for the title of stalker."

"Lesson learned," he said quickly. "But I think you're selling the personal shopper I hired a little short. She does have a degree in her field."

"In shopping?" Sabra questioned. "Isn't that an urban legend or an urban princess's fantasy?"

Sabra leaned onto the bed with on one knee, his body beckoning to her again, but her belly rumbled.

He chuckled, the sound more relaxed than she recalled hearing from him before.

"Maybe." He grabbed his jeans and stepped into them. "All I really cared about is her ability to accurately judge her client's size and taste from the pictures provided."

"You gave someone pictures of me?" The concept was actually less alarming than the idea that he had pictures of her.

He shrugged before reaching for her hand and clasping it.

"The shopping is limited up here, Sabra. Since I wasn't going to give you too much time to think about getting on the plane, I wanted to make sure I had what you needed when you got here."

He pulled her toward the kitchen and left her in front of the huge island that made up the outer edge of the cooking area. It had a dark marble slab on top and eight barstools completed the breakfast bar.

Tarak walked confidently through the kitchen and pulled a skillet out of a cabinet. Next he opened the huge side-by-side refrigerator and removed some bread, milk, and eggs.

"You know your way around a kitchen?" she asked, surprised.

"Why so surprised?" He broke the eggs on the edge of a glass mixing bowl and tossed the shells in a trash bin. "Doesn't cooking fit the image you have of me?"

She climbed up onto one of the stools. It had a plush back and padded seat. "Not unless it's a fresh kill being roasted over a campfire."

He laughed at her while beating the eggs. A splash of milk, and a sprinkle of nutmeg and cinnamon completed the batter. He pulled two thick slices of bread from the package and soaked them. A stainless-steel coffeemaker sat off to one side of the range, and he filled it with efficient motions. The scent of ground coffee rose up to tease her nose.

"I think I may have exhausted my quota of uncivilized behavior for the day." He dropped a dab of butter into the pan and angled it around so the hot surface was evenly coated. "At least until you're fed."

He filled a kettle and sat it on a back burner. Once he'd placed the bread in the skillet, he moved to one of the cabinets and returned with a box of her favorite tea.

"You know me better than I know you." Maybe it wasn't the wisest thing to say out loud, because she was admitting a weakness.

He shrugged before turning the French toast. "That's my fault. Success has a way of attracting insincere people, so I tend to check up on people I let in my life."

"And you've learned to keep your personal information private."

He slid the finished toast onto a plate and delivered it to her with a flourish.

"I can't have my epic cooking skills becoming well-known. I do have a company to run."

The kettle was whistling and he turned around to fill a mug with steaming water.

"Or have your cutthroat image doubted?"

He placed the mug in front of her. "Exactly."

The toast was a perfect golden brown and smelled delicious. She spread around the butter he'd topped it with before pouring a little syrup on it. It was real maple syrup, and the first taste was amazing.

He was busy fixing himself a batch while she contemplated the fact that Tarak Nektosha was actually making breakfast.

"I guess cooking skills come in handy up here."

He nodded before tossing his own breakfast onto a plate. He didn't join her at the bar, but leaned back against the countertop.

"I'm making you nervous," she observed.

He froze mid-chew, his eyes narrowing before he finished the bite in his mouth and swallowed. The coffee was finished and he filled a mug with the dark brew. But he stopped after one sip and just held the mug against his chest as he looked at her.

"I built this house out of a sense of revenge. It's a little odd to be inviting someone into it."

"Karma has a twisted sense of humor."

He snorted and flashed her one of those grins that made her insides melt. The guy was just too sexy.

She looked around the spacious kitchen but resisted the urge to look over her shoulder because she didn't want to break the spell of the moment. It was one of those rare moments when Tarak had his guard down and she desperately wanted to know what the man inside was like.

Maybe she'd find some sort of understanding about her reaction to him.

"Her name was Liluye and I was twenty when I asked her to marry me."

"That's young."

He took a long sip of coffee. "Not on reservation land. Kids get married all the time and divorced just as often. It's a screwed-up sort of thinking, that sex is more respectable under the bonds of matrimony even though you break those vows when the passion has cooled off. The bottom line is, I wanted to get into her bed."

"It sounds like it was something more if you built all this in revenge."

His eyes narrowed.

"I'd have to be pretty shallow not to notice, Tarak." She toyed with her tea bag for a moment. "But it can wait." She started to get up.

He drew in a deep breath before opening his eyes. "I want to finish this conversation."

Chapter 7

It was the word *conversation* that kept her on the barstool. Fuck buddies didn't have personal conversations.

"The ring I gave Liluye was worth about five hundred bucks. I spent all summer working for that cash."

"So you don't—"

"Come from money?" He tilted his head to one side. "Nope. I was reservation born and raised. The horse was more reliable than my dad's truck, when he was around. Which wasn't very often. I went to work at twelve to help feed the new baby he'd leave my mom with every time he showed up until she defied the church and got her tubes tied. Lightning didn't strike her dead, and there was a hell of a lot less stress in the house without another baby on the way."

"That explains the condom stress."

He nodded, his fingers white around the mug. "Kids need a father, not a dog who shows up because he's looking for a bitch who won't bite him."

"At least you had your mom. Single-parent households can be good ones."

"Like yours?"

He flipped the tone of conversation with two words. She felt her defenses rising and had to force herself not to shut him out. He was trying to adjust to her rules of giving more, so she'd have to find the guts to match his effort.

She swallowed the lump in her throat and nodded. "Yeah, like mine. My dad is awesome."

"And your mother?" he pressed her.

"Well…" Sabra shrugged. "I don't know much about her. She wanted a boy, and I guess the sonogram made me look like one, so she carried me. At least that's what I heard from my dad when he'd had enough whisky to forget his own rules about not darkening her name. Ninety-nine percent of the time he just said it didn't work out but that he was the lucky one because he had me."

"That's a hell of a standard for a man to impose on himself." Tarak drew another sip of coffee before nodding. "I think I admire him."

"Good, because he's going to be a little pissed that I didn't call him before coming up here," she admitted. "And I'm not talking about being pissed at me. He's the kind of man who expects you to shake his hand before taking his daughter out of state. He's going to make you pay for it if you two ever meet."

Tarak grinned. "I'd admire him more for it. What's your mother's deal with only wanting a boy?"

"My mother is the granddaughter of Giovanni Greci."

"As in the political family Greci?" Tarak's tone had sharpened.

"So I understand. Apparently, there was an inheritance promised to the first grandson. That didn't turn out to be me. Since males control the sex of the unborn child, she used that as the excuse to go back home and make up with her family for running off with an American soldier."

He smiled, looking surprised. "Amazing. You realize you could get some serious hush money?"

It was her turn to narrow her eyes. "I'll make my way. I've got my dad, and if my mom wants to forget she fell in love with an American, well, she's the one who missed out on getting to be part of our lives. Because it was and is great." She got down from the barstool. "I'm going to get a shower."

It wasn't a total retreat, but there was definitely a lack of courage on her part. She felt exposed, which ticked her off because she really did love her life. Maybe when she was a little girl she'd longed for a mommy, but maturity had helped her grow past that. Okay and the one time she'd mentioned it to her dad, he'd put on a frilly apron and wig and cooked supper in it. The memory still made her giggle.

Tarak caught up with her and took her hand. The firm grip was emotionally shattering. She loved it yet hated feeling like she needed it. Her emotions were all twisted and making absolutely no sense.

"Okay, shower and then I want to show you something."

He led her to a bathroom that was off to the side of the master bedroom. On the way in, he stopped and pushed some controls on the wall.

"The tile will warm up in a few minutes."

There was a small gas-burning fireplace in the bathroom as well. He turned a long key and it lit with a blue flash.

"For such a remote area, you sure do have the best of modern conveniences."

"The house and testing facility are completely self-contained. I have three people in charge of making sure we have all the resources necessary. It's that big of a job up here. Summer is a busy time."

Her attention shifted to the shower. It was massive, enclosed in glass, a walk-in type that had granite tile. There were water jets set into the walls and five showerheads up high. He stripped out of his jeans and walked in to turn it on. Once the water was pouring over his hard form, he pushed his wet hair back and grinned at her.

"Come try out the shower, Sabra."

"Said the snake to the mouse."

He chuckled and grabbed a soap bar. It lathered up, spreading bubbles over his skin as he rubbed it across his trim waist. "I see you as more of a snake charmer."

He walked back under one of the showerheads and closed his eyes as the water hit him in the face.

It was far too tempting to resist. She tore off her clothing and joined him while his eyes were still closed. She took the soap bar from his hand and began to wash him. He turned and flattened his hands against the granite tile, granting her full access to his body.

She intended to take full advantage of the moment too. The fact that he was letting her have her way didn't matter. There was a challenge that filled her—she wanted to make him enjoy it enough to give her control more often.

There was also the blunt fact that he was *sexy* in capital letters, and she loved every moment of being able to touch him.

She finished his back and slid the soap bar over his tight buns. Ducking under one of his arms, she applied the soap to his chest. He had a light coating of crisp, dark hair on his chest that ended at his waist. But she went lower, until she'd found the hair above his cock.

"Ummmm… and now to the snake-charming part," she purred in a voice that was far more sultry than she recalled being able to pull off.

He opened his eyes and watched her. The water was already warm, but she was heating up too. There were times she could feel his gaze on her. It was unlike anything she'd ever experienced, the pure erotic feeling of it. She drew the soap bar along his length and then bent her knees so she could wash his legs.

He growled softly. She looked up and gave him a smile that promised him no mercy.

"Bitch," he labeled her with a note of approval in his voice.

She came back up his body and cupped his cock between her breasts.

"*Shit.*"

He was still coated in soap, so their skin was slippery. He thrust forward, using her cleavage.

"That's fucking hot, Sabra."

He arched back and she used her forearms to keep her breasts pressed inward. She heard his breathing growing more labored and leaned forward to lick the head of his cock when it emerged near her face.

"Crap!" He jerked and lost control. A thick spurt of come shot out at her face but she didn't care. She reached down and grabbed his balls, stroking them as he continued to ejaculate.

He leaned on the wall again, only this time there was a faint tremble running along his legs. His eyes were closed as he drew in raspy breaths.

"I thought you'd wash the soap off first."

"And give you warning?" She stood up and stroked his cock to loosen the lather still clinging to it. "Hell no. It was my turn to break you, Mr. Nektosha."

His eyes sprang open. "Tarak." He cupped the back of her head and held her captive. "Don't fucking call me that. Call me your lover, your boyfriend, or even an asshole when it applies, but never Mr. Nektosha." He pressed a hard kiss against her mouth. It was bold and demanding too. He thrust his tongue deep inside her mouth, thrusting and stroking the velvet surface of her own.

He massaged her nape, his fingers working at the knots she hadn't realized were there.

"I've never involved myself with an employee, but I just couldn't help myself." He swiped the soap bar from the floor and began to wash her.

"I think it's fair to say I'm a step up from Anastasia."

He turned her around so he could wash her back. But she could feel the tension between them.

She'd opened a can of worms now.

"She's one of those things you can call me an asshole for. I wanted sex but didn't want to risk getting into a relationship where I might have to share part of myself. Her father does a lot of business with me. It seemed logical."

"But relationships should be about happiness."

He was rubbing her back aggressively, creating a thick lather with his quick motions. Sabra turned around and let the water from one of the showerheads hit her back.

"I think she was using you just as much."

"That doesn't make me less of an asshole."

He smoothed the soap along her sides and over the curves of her hips.

"Yeah, well, we're both guilty of not wanting to be alone."

He bent down and applied the soap to her legs. Little bolts of delight began racing up her body, intent on derailing her thoughts altogether in favor of redirecting her attention to the growing need bubbling inside her.

"Is that an admission about the state of affairs between you and one Kevin Guterman?"

She choked on a snicker. "He took my suggestion of adding a little erotic foreplay and spanked me with a flip-flop on the beach in front of his football buddies."

Tarak's lips thinned. "Did you ask him to dominate you?"

He ran the soap bar over one cheek of her bottom. Her eyes widened as her clit gave a crazy twist. She rolled her lips inward because even with the water from the shower raining down on them, they felt dry.

"The point is, I was holding onto a relationship that wasn't satisfying. That was what we were talking about."

"Hmm…" He soaped up her other cheek. "Was it?" He dropped the soap bar and turned her around to face the wall. He captured her wrists and pressed her hands flat on the dark granite surface while holding his body against her from head to toe. "I'd like to address the topic of domination."

She tried to turn around but only succeeded in pushing herself against his body. "I wasn't asking him for domination."

Tarak leaned down and bit the side of her neck. Once again, the little nip sent a shudder down her back, one he felt because he was pressed against her.

"Would you ask me?"

He cupped her hips, holding her still as his dark suggestion bounced around inside her head.

"No… um…"

"Ummm…" He smoothed his hand over one of her buttocks, making every inch of her skin feel as though she were in some sort of heightened sensory mode. "I won't use a flip-flop."

She flipped around and ducked under his arm.

"It was just a last-ditch effort to make something work that wasn't. I thought it was the sex. I was wrong." She needed something to do, something other than continuing the discussion about domination. Her mind was flatly rebelling against the idea; Tarak was already a dominant enough force in her life.

But her body was melting.

She grabbed a bottle of shampoo and turned it over. The gel pooled in her hand and she began to work it through her wet hair. When she closed her eyes to rinse it, he moved up and began to massage the shampoo out of her hair.

She shivered, craving him but at the same time being uncomfortable with her reactions to him.

When the shampoo was rinsed away, he turned her and kissed her again. He started soft, teasing her lips before pressing her to open her mouth for him. He stroked her back, the water making their skin so much slicker. When he made it to her lower back, he stroked out to her hips and clasped them.

A jolt went through her when he did. There was something

about the hold that just made her pussy heat up. He lifted his head and his lips curled.

"I can smell you again."

"You're going to make me self-conscious."

He shook his head and sat down on the large seat at the far end of the shower. "You like me the way I am. The scent of your pussy drives me insane. You like it when I tell you I notice the scent." His eyes glittered with challenge. "Come here and top me."

It was a demand—a dominant one. Somehow, he was turning a submissive position into something dominant. It surprised the hell out of her, but she was moving toward him before she finished thinking. He offered her a hand to help her mount him. His cock stood up straight, and he grabbed her hips, steadying her when she balanced on one knee to move her other thigh over him.

The head of his cock burrowed between the open lips of her slit. It felt like she'd been waiting forever for penetration. Even while she realized it was overly dramatic, she still let out a soft cry as she sheathed him.

"Again, Sabra."

Her eyes opened wide, and she sat still at the tone in his voice. He stroked one side of her bottom, and she rose up too fast. She was all the way off his cock before she controlled her reaction.

He chuckled and pulled her back into position by her hips. "You respond so honestly."

His cock brushed her opening again and she sank down onto it. "You sound as if you've had experience with…"

He gave her a light smack on the bottom and she shot back up. "Why is the word stuck in your throat, Sabra?"

She kept enough control to keep herself from lifting too far up this time. She plunged back down faster, hoping to distract him, but his eyes remained hard and controlled.

"Why?" he demanded again.

She tried to lift herself up, but he held her down, his cock filling her to bursting. He leaned forward and nuzzled her neck while she tried to rise.

"Tell me why."

It was no longer a question.

"I don't know."

He kissed her neck and then bit her earlobe. "Yes you do."

Her clit was driving her insane. She needed to come, needed to fuck him, but he held her completely still, frustrating her beyond endurance.

"I don't know," she spat at him. "I guess it's just me wondering if I want domination or if I'm just jumping on board the latest trend." She rose off him with more force, gaining her freedom. But once she'd pressed back down on his length, she paused. "Maybe you're just bored with sex kittens and want a new kink."

Celeste certainly thinks so.

"A valid argument."

She hadn't been expecting him to agree with her. It took the pressure off and allowed her confidence to build. She could put herself completely at his mercy, but he wasn't insisting.

She rose and fell, moving faster and faster. She ignored the burning in her thighs and used his shoulders to keep her balance. He kept his hands on her hips, guiding her as he began to lift up off the seat to meet every downward plunge. His jaw was clenched, but he held back, waiting for her to peak. The moment she did, he growled and took control of the pace.

He stood and pressed her up against the wall and drove his cock into her body with a hard rhythm. She hadn't finished when he started to come. For a moment she was caught in the storm of sensation, held completely within its grasp. Once it ebbed, she felt completely spent. Standing was even questionable.

Tarak held her up and they both showered again.

"Your water bill is going to be outrageous."

"It's all snow melt. There are no city utilities here. Most of the homes up here have outhouses, and you'd better remember to take a rifle with you because there are bears."

"Charming."

He shut off the shower and offered her a towel. The moment the warm water stopped flowing, she hurried closer to the fireplace. The tiles had indeed warmed up, and she smiled as she wiggled her toes. A phone started buzzing in the office set off to the other side of the master bedroom.

Of course he had an office next to his bedroom.

"The closet on the right is yours. Make a list of anything you need."

Tarak tucked a towel around his waist and braved the chill beyond the bathroom. For a moment she felt abandoned.

Please…

She shook it off, determined not to act like a lost little girl. Tarak answered the call, his deep voice poised and professional.

Well, whoever was on the other end of the line didn't know he was only wearing a towel.

That little bit of knowledge restored her confidence. He wasn't a man who let distractions into his private space. Their breakfast conversation made it clear she was the only woman he'd had in the cabin, and that spoke volumes about how deep his own feelings ran—even if she was unsure about just what feelings she harbored for him.

Well, she was there to discover the answer.

Sabra turned to look at the other side of the bathroom. A huge full-length mirror was capped on each side with doorways. She headed for the right side and the lights came on the moment she crossed the threshold.

It was a woman's dream. The closet was bigger than her master bedroom. There were drawers and closet space and shoe racks and storage-space shelving. More than a dozen garments were hung up and she looked through them.

All right, the professional shopper did know her stuff. Most of the garments would fit her and they were also in flattering cuts for her figure. She opened one of the drawers and looked at the bras. Sabra couldn't help but smile at the multitude of sizes. It took a woman to understand how tricky bra sizing was.

She selected one that was right and tried it on. Another drawer yielded underwear, and just like the bras, there was a selection of styles and sizes. Turning around, she tried to decide what to wear. There were soft, comfortable-looking tunics and leggings. A yawn caught her off guard as jet lag began to take its revenge. She tossed the bra back in the drawer and grabbed sweat pants and a T-shirt.

Back in the bathroom, she found a drawer full of toiletries. A quick pass with a hairbrush and toothbrush and she was wandering back into the master bedroom. Tarak was talking on the phone somewhere beyond the master bedroom double doorway.

She yawned again but hesitated before she surrendered to the need to lie down.

I've had sex with the guy like a dozen times!

Yeah, but there was still something very intimate about crawling into his bed.

It was a really nice bed though.

The sheets were flannel and cozy. The pillows were soft and plentiful. She pushed the comforters around and smelled one to discover they were silk filled. She smiled as she drifted off into sleep, happy to know she wouldn't need an allergy med because they were goose down.

Tarak had enough of an effect on her; the man didn't need to see her with a swollen nose.

Someone was holding her.

Sabra surfaced from sleep to wonder who had his arm draped around her waist.

Kevin wasn't a snuggler.

But it felt really good. She turned and inhaled the scent of his skin, sighing when she recognized Tarak. She wasn't really awake, didn't want to be, but she wanted to feel him holding her. He pulled her closer and inhaled the scent of her hair. He tangled his legs with hers as he settled into the bed. Her cheek ended up against his chest and the beat of his heart filled her head.

Now this was something more.

―ᴡ―

Her cell phone woke her.

It began playing the opening song from *Ride of the Valkyries* from where she'd left her purse on top of her bag. Sabra sat up but bumped into someone on the way, smacking her head on Tarak's chin and cussing.

"Exactly," he agreed.

She covered her mouth like a kid. He rubbed a hand over his jaw and glared at her.

"So you cuss. I do too," Tarak observed in a groggy voice.

Her phone had stopped but it started up again. "That's my dad. I forgot to call him." She looked at the clock. "Yesterday," she groaned.

"You were out like a light."

Tarak flipped the bedding back and walked over to her purse. He tossed her cell phone to her and headed into the bathroom. The sink faucet started running a moment later.

She drew her finger across the screen and pushed the redial.

"About time you answered."

"Hey, Dad. Sorry."

"You sound half awake." Her dad honed in on the sound of her voice. "It's past eleven."

"I'm in a different time zone. It's only eight here."

"Is that so?" her father mused. "Now I know I've got a bad heart, but I don't remember being senile."

"You're not, Dad. It was a very last-minute thing. I'm in Alaska at the Nektosha testing facility." She tried to make it sound completely work related.

"Celeste might have mentioned something about that."

Her cover was totally blown.

"Dad—"

"Don't use that tone, Sabra Sunshine," her father reprimanded her with his favorite nickname from her childhood. It was worse than her middle name because when he called her Sabra Sunshine, he was worried.

She hated worrying her daddy. "I'm fine."

"Don't tell me fish stories. I know a thing or two about falling hard for someone who is out of your category in life."

"I know you do, but I need to see this through."

There was a parental grunt of doubt on the other end of the line.

"Really, Daddy, I want to see if there is more to this."

There was a long pause on the other end of the line. "All right, Princess Sunshine. Just remember, call me anytime you need a plane ticket home. I want your word that you will get yourself to an airport and call me if there's a problem."

"I promise, but only if you tell me what the second doctor says about your heart."

"Damn. You're just like your old man," her father grumbled.

"Take it or leave it," Sabra warned. "But I think it's fair to warn you that Celeste spills information my way too."

"Damn," her father grunted. "It's a deal."

"You'll tell me, as soon as you know?" she clarified.

"Yes. You nosy child."

"Thanks, Dad."

She pushed the end button and looked up. Tarak was leaning in the doorway. He had a grin on his lips that looked almost bemused, until she looked at the rest of him. Every inch of him was solid and hard and completely bare. His expression tightened, darkening with hunger, but he held back.

"Get some jeans on. I've got something to show you, Sabra."

"I like what you're showing me right now." His cock looked delicious.

His eyes narrowed. "Flatterer. Get dressed. It's important, and I cleared my morning so we could spend it together."

"Okay, I feel special."

He shrugged but denied her any further details. She found jeans in the closet and cozy, squishy socks to keep her toes warm. Once she was dressed, she went back to the mudroom and put her snow pants on.

"Where are we going?"

He finished knotting his boot lace and offered her an unreadable expression.

"To my past."

―⁓―

"The snow will be melting soon."

Tarak was driving this time. The front of the Terrain Tank was a feast for her inner child. There was an interactive touch screen computer with access to the conditions around them.

"Damned storm rolled in right after I got here and made me wait to get you here."

She turned to stare at him.

"I told you I couldn't stop thinking about you, Sabra. I wanted you up here Tuesday."

"You could have called."

He was keeping his attention on the road, but she saw his knuckles turning white.

"I should have," he admitted at last. "It was a risk I wasn't willing to expose myself to. I wanted to see if you went back to Kevin."

It was an admission.

"You have trust issues."

He cut her a quick glance, but it was enough to curl her toes. There was a current between them, one that was so intense it shocked them both whenever they were close.

Neither of them was comfortable with it though.

The road was bumpy, but the Terrain Tank crawled through it like sand. The snow crunched but the sky was clear. The forest ahead of them had lots of trees which had already lost their coating of snow. The temperature displayed on the dash computer was a nice round forty degrees.

"It's beautiful up here."

He turned and grinned at her as though she were telling him his favorite spot could become hers as well. They drove on, passing trucks and other four-wheel-drive vehicles. Along the side of the road, teams of dogs pulled a sled by every so often, the dogs yelping as they ran through the two-foot-high snow.

"But it is sort of killing my ideas that puppies go with grass."

He chuckled. "You might not want to say that around the locals. They take those dogs up onto the glaciers during the summer months to train them for the Iditarod. Most of them were born up on the ice."

That explained the happy expressions on the dogs' faces. Okay, maybe that was a stretch, but the dogs did look as though they were having fun. The few stopped sleds she saw had dogs that howled and pawed at the ground eagerly.

"Will it paint an 'outsider' label on my forehead?"

"Something like that." He turned off the main road and the snow started crunching beneath the oversized tires again. "Don't ask me how I know that."

"That's right, you said you were reservation raised. You mean the one in—"

"Arizona," he finished with his attention solidly on the road. It was little more than a lane cut through the wilderness, and the forest wasn't too keen on it. Young saplings were growing up on the sides of the road, trying to cover the cleared ground.

They kept going, and the grade increased, but the Terrain Tank handled it with ease.

"I'm beginning to see why you make these kinds of vehicles."

"You're actually spot on," he answered. "Once I had the money to choose what I wanted to do with my life, I looked around for a need people would pay to fulfill. Around here, that's rough and tough equipment that can take the environment on and keep going."

"Like you." It just slipped out, but she wasn't sorry, because his reaction pleased her. His lips twitched up before he made a sharp turn and headed up an even narrower road.

"It's been a while since I came up here." His voice had become pensive. "Even longer since I wanted to share it with anyone."

In the distance, the trees thinned out. Tarak headed for a huge clearing that had what looked like a ghost town from some Western movie in it. Piles of dirt and rock were covered with melting snow. A long conveyer belt ran along one side of the clearing, a broken-down earthmover sitting next to a pile of dirt near it. A few old buildings completed the site, the tin roofing rusted.

He pulled up and cut the engine. For a long moment, he gripped the steering wheel and stared at the earthmover.

"Liluye was Apache. She sold my ring and married another member of the tribe. "

Horror choked her for a moment. "What a cold-hearted bitch. But it explains the trust issues."

"It was also a source of shame for her family." He opened the door and climbed out. He stopped and pulled a rifle from the backseat and took a moment to make sure it was loaded. He looked up to see her watching him uncertainly.

"There's some big wildlife up here in Alaska. If you're staying, you're going to have to learn how to fire one of these."

"My dad taught me how to use a firearm."

He gave her a skeptical look.

Sabra pushed her own door open and joined him in front of the Terrain Tank. He'd slung the rifle over his shoulder before he looked at the quiet buildings. But to him, they weren't silent. She could see him listening to his memories as he looked around.

"This was a worn-out gold mine that Liluye's grandfather owned. When we were growing up, he'd sit around and tell us about all the gold he was going to dig out of this ground when he got back up here. He always made an excuse to avoid doing that."

Tarak began walking beside the long conveyer belt. The snow crunched under Sabra's boots as she kept up.

"The whole family wanted me to disappear. They gave my name to military recruiters, but I wasn't interested." He stopped when they could see the roof of a small cabin. It was set up on pillars with a small, rough plank porch. The door was just as primitive looking.

"Her grandfather finally summoned me, and that meant I couldn't ignore him, because he was my elder. Nartan went with me to see him. You might remember him from Angelino's. We're like brothers."

"That explains the ice wine."

A little glimmer of satisfaction flickered in his eyes. "Liluye's grandfather wanted me to leave, so Liluye could settle into her marriage. He claimed I was upsetting her and she was pregnant. I could have told him to go to hell, the reservation was my home too, but I remembered his tales about this mine." Tarak sent her a bemused look. "I should have been suspicious at how quickly he agreed to sign this claim over to me."

He marched on toward the steps. He took a moment to test each step before putting his full weight on it. One creaked but it held, so she followed him up. The door wasn't locked, but the knob was stiff.

"Rule of the wilderness is to leave stuff unlocked in case someone is caught out in the elements. Shelter means the difference between life and death." He had to duck beneath the doorframe and took a good look around before allowing her inside. "I cooked more than one fresh kill over that fire."

The fireplace in question was a small one. There was an iron spike running through the center of it, and the bricks it was made of were black with soot.

"So Nartan and I came up here, drunk on childhood stories of getting rich easy."

"Are you saying you made your money in gold?" she asked incredulously.

"Fate has a crooked sense of humor at times." He kicked a stump that was sitting on the floor by a rough-looking table. The top of the stump was worn smooth, proving it had served as a seat. The cabin itself was only twenty feet by twenty feet. There was a kitchen in one corner, if you were generous enough to call a stove and three-foot-long counter space a kitchen. A single cabinet hung on the wall over the counter, and it was made of plywood with only holes for handles. Across the bare board floor there were two bunks built into the wall, the mattresses wrapped in huge plastic bags.

It was a far cry from the magnificent cabin she'd spent the night in.

"We worked this claim for three years. Two other boyhood friends came with Nartan and me. They chewed me out more than once for my stubborn refusal to throw in the towel. The truth was, I didn't want to go back home, back to being the overthrown fiancé. An Indian reservation is a tight-knit community. I wasn't going back until I'd made something of myself."

He turned his back on the cabin and walked back outside. She joined him as he surveyed the rest of the ghost town. He lifted a hand and pointed at the earthmover.

"I spent endless hours in that thing over those three years. The moment the snow melted enough for us to mine pay dirt, we were digging."

"I guess I can see how you got in shape."

He grinned at her. "One thing Alaska has lots of is fish. You need water to run the wash plant… that thing over there. It shakes the dirt, separating the heavier gold and washing the dirt away. When we weren't mining, we were fishing."

"I guess the original owner was pretty upset when you pulled a haul out of this claim."

"He laughed at us," Tarak replied. "At Nartan and me for sticking it out past the first year. For the first two years, we pulled out just enough to buy fuel for the machines. It was a battle every month to see if we had the money to buy fuel for the next month. Those were mighty long years. We lived off the land completely. Our clothing wore off us. I understand we became the town joke."

"I think they misjudged your tenacity."

He shrugged and went down the steps. "I think I developed a lot of it right here. That outhouse was sure a test of character in the middle of winter, but I preferred it to returning to the reservation."

She looked up the way and saw the small building in question. It was uphill and a good thirty feet from the cabin. "I bet that is a long walk in the snow—a *really* long walk."

He nodded. "The seat is mighty cold too."

She shivered, earning a chuckle from him. He jerked his head in the direction of the far side of the camp. They trudged through the snow and, where the snow was gone, through patches of mud. He offered her a hand and tugged her up to what looked like the very edge of camp. When she made it to the top, she could look down on a massive dug-out pit. It was full of snow and looked like a giant's cereal bowl.

"There is where I pulled my future out of the ground." His voice was full of accomplishment. He was staring at the pit, locked into the memory. "We found what had once been the base of a waterfall. It's what every prospector dreams of coming across, but there is no way to predict where they will be. It's fate."

"And the reward for the tenacious."

He turned to look at her. For a moment, need shone in his eyes, but this was a far different type of need than what she was accustomed to seeing in the black orbs. He craved her approval, wanted to hear the praise in her voice. She didn't think she'd ever seen him truly happy before, but at that moment, he was.

And he was sharing it with her.

"You should have seen Nartan and my faces when we dumped that first load of pay dirt on the wash station. Prior to that, we'd been pulling in flecks of gold that we carefully collected in a jar. This time though, once the water took the dirt away, we had nuggets the size of jelly beans. This single hole gave me everything I needed to start Nektosha. Nartan wanted out of the wilderness and used his share to open his restaurants. He said something about never eating a blackened rabbit again."

"And you?" she asked quietly. "You discovered that money couldn't buy peace."

His expression tightened. "I think you are the only person besides Nartan that I'd put up with hearing that from."

He'd closed himself off again. She felt the wall going up and witnessed the guarded look entering his eyes. He turned and walked back through the camp without another word.

It was devastating to see because she realized there was no hope for anything more between them so long as he held on to the bitter past.

His heart was still broken.

That was why he had it on ice.

Tarak drove straight to the Alaskan office and disappeared after he gave her a quick introduction to her new workplace. It was a long row of window offices that overlooked the test track and airfield. The entire building was curved, built into the granite cauldron the site sat in. It was a huge U-shaped valley a glacier had carved out in centuries past. Here and there, a massive boulder sat where the melting ice flow had dropped it.

When she looked up the hill to the mountains surrounding them, there were faint glimpses of more glaciers.

It was a kick-ass view. Maybe not the one she'd been coveting on the sixteenth floor of the West Coast towers, but it was definitely breathtaking.

The office manager took one look at Tarak's closed office door before turning around to deal with her.

"Let's find you a desk," Kurt Thompson muttered. "We're as posh as the West Coast towers in an Alaskan sort of way."

"Does that mean there isn't an outhouse?" she asked hopefully.

Kurt laughed. "You're going to fit right in. You know, it's the permafrost that causes the problem with putting in a sewer system. The ground is frozen year round, about three feet down in a lot of places. That's why the cabin and many of the buildings are on pillars. The heat from the house would melt the permafrost and sink the structure."

He led her to an empty office. "All your passwords will work on the system, but I'll be changing your projects over to ones we're handling here. It's nearly impossible to get a female up here, and I've got a mountain of things I need your perspective on. I'm going to need you over in design and development to do some hands-on with everything from steering wheels to seat cushions."

"Sounds good." She slid into the chair behind the desk.

"Along with the lack of female office staff goes a lack of secretaries. Kitchen is down on the right for coffee. The cook will make whatever you want because there is nothing in the way of restaurants nearby."

Self-contained.

Tarak's words rose from her memory.

I built this house out of a sense of revenge.

At least he was honest about his demons, but boy did the man have them. It was almost overwhelming. A sense of defeat threatened to flatten her beneath its weight.

No.

Nope.

She was not going to let it trample her. She'd understood the odds of any sort of relationship working out between them. So the choices were to let him keep his ghosts or to do something to break through the ice holding his heart captive.

She realized exactly what it needed to be too. Since the sex appeal was what had brought them together, she'd have to remove it to see if there was anything else for them to do. She knew one thing for sure and that was that she didn't need to be involved in another relationship that was merely convenient. Tarak wasn't the only one whose happiness counted. She was in it for her own too. She just wished the odds weren't stacked so high against her, but the look in his eyes up at the mine hadn't been promising.

Yet the fact that he'd taken her there was a hopeful sign.

It was a bold risk, but hell, Alaska was the place for risks paying off.

She sighed, pulling her chair closer to her desk and ordering herself to focus on the daily grind. Tarak Nektosha was just as mysterious as the day she'd met him.

It was just possible that was what drew her to him.

His calendar was full.

Brimming, in fact. If he needed to take a leak, he'd fall behind.

There were IMs stacking up along the lower part of his screen as the top of the hour approached, and with it the promise of another critical conference call.

All he wanted to do was check in on Sabra.

It was a nagging little impulse that made him smile even as he felt the burn of frustration. The testing site was his private playground. In ten years, he'd never invited a single female onto the site. Anastasia had whined to her billionaire father about it for months.

Three minutes to call time.

He sat down and moved his mouse over the IM menu.

How's the office?

Sabra jumped when the IM popped up on her screen with a soft chime. Her lips split with a wide smile that she quickly mastered before looking around for a webcam, but there didn't seem to be one.

It's great.

She felt like a teenager with her first texting privileges.

Got a conference call in one minute.

Okay.

She stared at the single word reply and realized how little it revealed.

Thanks for the chat.

It wasn't much of a chat, unless she recalled that he'd already blown off a good portion of the day with her. He was Nektosha after all. It was touching in a way she'd never thought possible. The time on her computer changed to show the top of the hour. She stared at the open chat bubble for a full five minutes before closing it.

Celeste was right. Tarak was a dangerous man but the true threat he posed was to her heart.

—◦◦◦—

Tarak was distracted.

The first few minutes of his call passed in a blur as he watched the chat bubble. He tried to focus on business but held off from closing the link. The lack of self-control annoyed him, but he still couldn't bring himself to close the link. When Sabra cut the line, he noted the time and discovered himself grinning, an insane rush of giddiness pulling him out of the workday and suspending him in the moment with Sabra.

But the conference call was in full swing.

"Yes, I'm listening…"

But later, well later, he'd be free to explore his fascination with Sabra.

Chapter 8

KURT KNOCKED ON HER wall just after five.

"Boss man told me to give you a lift back to the cabin."

He leaned in the open door and grinned at her. The lack of formality was refreshing. She suddenly realized how formal and stale the West Coast office really was. Sure she wanted her career, but she didn't want to pay the price of losing herself and forgetting why she worked so hard in the first place.

She wanted to enjoy the things she liked.

"Yeah, thanks."

Kurt waited for her to get her jacket. He was a middle-aged man, and he smiled at her jovially.

Alaska. Population male.

Kurt drove her back up to the cabin. "Don't go walking without a rifle. The bears are starting to wake up. And they're hungry."

"Thanks for the warning." She did appreciate it, but she wasn't going anywhere.

If she wanted more from her relationship with Tarak, she was realizing she'd have to give more too. The man ran a multi-trillion dollar empire; there was no way he cleared the office door at five sharp.

—◦◦◦—

The kitchen was stocked with everything a gourmet cook needed. There were top-of-the-line pans and knives. Opening the cabinets revealed an impressive stock of ingredients spanning from the basics, like flour, to the most exotic spices on the face of the planet.

The freezer was stocked with meat, and the refrigerator had all the fresh ingredients she could wish for. She started the microwave on a defrost cycle to thaw some meat and pulled out the other things she wanted. On impulse she reached for her private cell phone and sent Tarak a text message.

> You may have built this kitchen out of revenge but I'm going to show you how to use it correctly. Dinner is on in an hour.

The pans heated up quickly and soon the sound and smell of onions sautéing in butter filled the kitchen. She hummed as she added things to the pan, learning her way around the kitchen as she kept on top of three burners at the same time.

"You're sexy when you cook."

She turned to find Tarak leaning against the doorway. His cell phone was in his hand and his expression was guarded. The office dress code was far more rustic here. He had on a pair of jeans that suited his nature better.

A long-sleeved, button-down shirt was the only attempt he made at dressing up. Most of the other office staff wore turtlenecks or jersey-type shirts that were practical for the weather. Tarak's button-down had been pressed and set him just a little above the rest of the crowd. It even had cuff links.

That suited him too.

But he had left his boots behind in the entry room, giving her a peek at his socks. Somehow, those socks drove home the fact that she was in his private domain. The idea unleashed a little shiver that went down her back, and instead of being shocked, she savored the sensation. She was exactly where she wanted to be.

"I think I like your idea of what this kitchen is for better than my motivation for building it," he informed her.

She wiped her hands on a dish towel and went to him. He watched her as he might a snake, but she grabbed the cell phone and used her hold on his hand to pull him down for a quick kiss.

"Yes, you do," she whispered before moving back to check dinner. "Lucky for you I don't scare off so easily."

She could feel him watching her. It made her nervous, but she pulled in a deep breath to steady her nerves.

No guts, no glory.

"Wash up."

It was tempting to look over her shoulder to see what he was making of her taking control, but she resisted.

Be the rock, girl.

There was only one way to earn the respect of a man like Tarak and that was to face him head on. It might end in a fiery crash, but they always found a way to use that heat too.

She heard him snort before he stomped across the floor and disappeared inside the small powder room next to the entryway.

"Can I look forward to this kind of summons every night?"

She used a pot holder to pull the rolls from the oven and carried them to the table. "Only if you're lucky. I cook for people I care about and that's it. Never for Mr. Nektosha."

He snapped his jaw shut and raked a hand through his hair. "I'm being a control jerk."

"Elephant size," she confirmed on her way back to the range. The skillet had browned their dinner to golden perfection and she dished it up. "The sex is not what needs figuring out between us. That means we need to spend time doing something other than being naked."

She sat down and felt her confidence waver. She'd played her hand. All she could do was wait for him to decide how to respond.

He pulled his chair back and sat down. "You're right. That's why I took you up to the mine."

"I noticed."

"But I do like you naked."

She rolled her eyes.

He drew in a deep breath and his stern expression cracked a little. "This smells good."

"You've got a mean kitchen setup, so if it doesn't taste good, the fault is all mine." She cut into hers and tasted it.

Tarak made a little smacking sound with his lips before she finished swallowing. "That's good. Really good."

She agreed but put another forkful in her mouth to keep herself from asking him again. Damned confidence needed to stick by her side.

"You know how to make bread?"

He was pulling apart a roll, steam rising from it.

"We were always on a budget, Dad and me. So we'd play restaurant Donovan. Gold stars were awarded to only the best creations. Although the gold star was often made of tinfoil wrapped over cardboard, but a star is a star." She fended off another wave of shyness. "I used to keep those stars in a shoebox. My dad just might still have that box too."

"I only made cookies when one of my brothers or sister brought home a one hundred percent on a test. An A didn't cut it. I demanded perfection because too many people were telling them they couldn't achieve it."

"Did it work?"

"I put every last one of them through college."

She lifted her gaze to lock with his. They were more alike than she'd imagined. Locked inside each of them was a kid who had struggled against the odds and still wondered if he had made it. She could see the reflection of her own demons in his eyes, and it made her shiver.

"Can we get naked now?" he asked roughly, emotion making his tone gravelly.

Her lips went dry and she nodded. "I thought you'd never ask."

A familiar flash of anticipation went through her as he stood and scooped her up. He carried her off to the bedroom, and she happily forgot about every detail of reality.

They ended up in a tangled mess, the bedding pulled loose and shoved onto the floor. Tarak sprawled on his back, but he wasn't sleeping. He stroked her. His fingers played through her hair, along her collarbone, and over her shoulder as his breathing returned to normal.

"You waited five minutes to close the IM."

Sabra turned to look at him. "You noticed?"

He nodded, the flicker of the master bedroom fireplace dancing off his eyes. The orange and red light bathed his body, giving her a fine view of his magnificent form. The glow of satisfaction was still warming her insides, but the sight of him began to turn her on again.

"You distracted me from a conference call."

She shrugged. "Write me up."

He rolled over and propped his head on his hand, his elbow resting beside her head. She reached up and slipped her hands into his hair. With a gentle tug, she pulled his head down to rest on her chest. She toyed with his hair, threading her fingers through the strands. The firelight felt like a time vortex, taking them back a century.

He cupped her breast, massaging it gently. Sabra closed her eyes and drifted off with his scent filling her senses.

~~~

He hadn't realized his life was missing anything.

Sabra's heartbeat filled his head, and he realized he was fighting the urge to cry.

He rolled over, rebelling against the idea that he needed anyone.

But the mattress felt cold and he scooped Sabra up, pulling her close. A sense of completeness filled him. It was so great, he marveled at the fact that he'd overlooked how empty he'd felt before.

He smoothed Sabra's hair back from her face before surrendering to sleep.

—⁓—

"Master Lee wants to know where you are," Celeste informed her the next morning. "You did make a promise not to quit."

"My job circumstances changed," Sabra defended herself as she took a sip of her morning tea. "Stop hiding behind him—and my dad for that matter."

Celeste clicked her tongue. "I'm not sorry about that. Plan on numerous calls and guilt-inducing voice mails if you stop picking up. You are in a dangerous situation."

"Only if you count the damage that might be done to my heart," Sabra admitted.

Celeste drew in a harsh breath. "Sabra, you cannot be falling for him."

"Since when do emotions obey the rules of common sense?" she demanded, but the truth was, she was trying to get to an understanding herself. "I don't know what I feel, just that I'm happier here than I was back home."

Celeste snorted. "You should never take your self-worth from being with a man."

"Agreed," Sabra shot back. "I'm talking about how I *feel*, and I think I'm affecting him the same way. He and Nartan were gold prospectors up here together. They weren't born rich."

"Well, that's a point in their favor, but it doesn't change the fact that they are used to getting what they want now," Celeste stated firmly. "Once you've had a taste of the good life, you'll do a lot to maintain that standard."

"Tarak gave me two hundred thousand dollars as insurance against losing my job."

There was silence on the other end of the line for a long moment. "That's not enough money for him to sweat losing it."

"But it is enough to cut through my argument of not continuing a relationship with him because I need to pay my mortgage," Sabra explained. "You know that's true."

"Okay, Sabra, I guess you've got a point. But you'd better send me a picture of your wrists right now, because if he's tying you up, I'm getting on a plane to come up there and kick his ass."

"I'm fine."

"So send me the picture and prove it."

Celeste cut the line, leaving her ultimatum hanging in the morning air. Sabra grumbled but turned her phone over and snapped a picture of her wrist.

"What are you doing?"

She dropped the phone and stared at Tarak as he approached from the master suite. One dark eyebrow rose as he swiped the phone off the table and looked at the picture.

"Sabra?" His tone was pure determination.

She could say it was nothing, make an excuse. But then she'd have to forfeit her own demand for openness between them.

"Celeste is just wanting a little confirmation that I'm fine. She has a few trust issues, well-founded ones unfortunately, and she saw the marks on my wrist before and—"

"The what?" he cut her off, grabbed her wrist, and turned it over as he inspected it.

"It was only a few pink marks, from the tie. They faded in a day or so."

He went deadly still. For a moment, she saw the warriors in his past who had killed to protect their people.

"It's no big deal," she insisted.

He pushed away from her, his face becoming a mask of self-directed fury. "It's a major fucking big deal, Sabra!"

"No it's not," she countered. "I wanted it as much as you did."

He was shaking his head, and it felt as though he were rejecting her. The pain was so intense, she lunged after him.

And he retreated.

It stunned her, freezing her in place as it felt as if the breath were being torn out of her lungs. She couldn't breathe, couldn't think beyond the look of revulsion in his eyes.

"It matters because I care about you, Sabra." He curled his lips back. "I care."

He took one long step and captured her. His arms closed around her and bound her against his hard body. Relief flooded her and tears eased from her eyes. He kissed each one, stroking her hair back with long motions.

"I care."

Kurt leaned on the horn outside the cabin. Tarak drew in a shaky breath, refusing to let her loose until he'd drawn a second one and regained his composure.

"The entire development team is on the track waiting for me," he ground out.

"Then we're not going to keep them waiting."

She stretched up and pressed a kiss against his chin. "I care too."

He shuddered and released her with a muffled curse and scooped up her cell phone from the table.

"We'll finish this tonight." But he stopped at the door. "Choose a safe word."

"I think that's a little extreme."

He stopped in the entry room doorway, blocking her exit from the house.

"You drive me crazy." His eyes narrowed and his lips thinned in a purely sexual way. "There are moments I'm consumed by getting inside you. But leaving a mark on you is completely unacceptable."

"It was probably my fault too." The memory of that moment, when she'd been twisting against the tie, was branded into her memory. "I was a little past thinking myself."

He cupped her chin, the touch gentle, but his gaze was brimming with rage. "I tied you up; the responsibility was mine."

"You're not going to budge on that, are you?"

"No," he bit out as he pushed through the door and sat down to put on his boots. "Choose the word."

"All right."

But there was part of her that didn't take solace in the promise. Instead, a tremor of excitement was building inside her.

———

The office was empty. Everyone had found an excuse to go over to the test track. She could see the test track from her office. The speedway-style track stretched over a half mile with different terrain styles for the Nektosha team to pit their creations against. There were huge snowblowers and rain machines. She heard the distant roar of engines revving up and watched new camouflage-painted vehicles take on the track.

The hangar doors were wide open, allowing the newest models out into the sunlight. Security was high too. Teams of armed men patrolled the entire perimeter to keep the press out. There was even a helicopter in the air.

Extreme.

She was beginning to think that was what *Nektosha* must mean in Apache. She was a little disappointed to discover that his name only meant *horse* and, in some cases, *little horse*. But she smiled as it dawned on her what it meant to him and his family—Tarak had been the jilted fiancé, but he'd grown into something far bigger and grander than the boy who had left home with a broken heart.

His words bounced around inside her head all day. Focusing became a difficult task she seemed to have little control over.

She never sent the picture to Celeste. Her relationship with Tarak was personal, and she wasn't willing to share it, even with her best girlfriend.

He cared.

The words had been torn from his soul. It was overly dramatic, but that didn't make her feel any differently. At least it fit with their relationship—everything in extremes. The afternoon crawled by, her belly knotting with anticipation.

Choosing a safe word just kept her mind on Tarak. It was a sort of mental torment. She tried to dismiss it, but it hounded her, sneaking around whatever project she was working on to tease her with the possibilities such a word could unleash in Tarak.

Be careful what you wish for.

Be careful what you decide not to try…

Kurt rapped on her door at five sharp. His eyes were sparkling and a good-natured grin was on his lips.

"You should get down to the track tomorrow. Everyone goes."

"Maybe."

They pulled up in front of the cabin and she set her teeth against her bottom lip as she went in and took her boots off. Submission had never been one of her turn-ons. But with Tarak, it was suddenly on the table. Giving him a safe word would be like handing him a permission slip that he could pull out anytime he pleased. She wasn't sure she could live with that possibility.

I'm not sure I can pass on the opportunity to let him have complete control.

Lord, she needed a drink.

She pushed the doors opened and froze. Music was playing

softly, filling the cabin. There wasn't a light on. Instead, the flicker of candlelight danced off the wood floors. One candle sat on the table, a single, long, white candle that illuminated a glass of white wine. A Post-it note was stuck to the surface of the table, drawing her close enough to read it.

"Put the garter belt on."

Her mouth went dry.

She looked around but Tarak was nowhere in sight, but she would swear she felt him watching her. It made her skin feel hot.

She lifted the wineglass and inhaled the aroma. It was thick and heady, almost making her dizzy. The candlelight made a golden pool around the edge of the table where the wine sat. She had to step into the light to read the note. She could feel him watching her, observing her from some dark shadow. For all the mental deliberating she'd done over playing submission games, the reality was very different.

She felt far more powerful than she'd expected. He might give her directions, but it was up to her if she wanted to obey them.

She took another sip of the wine before walking toward the bedroom. There were more candles burning on the dresser, and her garter belt was laid out on the bed. Another garment was there as well. She moved closer to identify it. Made of a soft blue silk, the corset was beautiful. Sabra reached out and touched it, smiling at how rich the fabric felt.

Excitement was making her jittery. She could still feel his eyes on her, and she wanted to make it worth his time. Scooping up the garter belt and corset, she went into the bathroom. There was one thing she wanted to do before slipping into the sexy garments.

She closed the door to the master bathroom and checked both closets before getting into the shower. When she was finished, every last pubic hair she had was gone. Sabra stared at her reflection, trying to decide if she liked the look. She wasn't sure. She shrugged and put the garter belt on before carefully pulling the stockings up her legs. The corset took a little more effort. She had to hug the two sides of it to her body while fiddling with the metal hooks that closed it. With no one to tighten the lace running down the back, she had to take it off and tighten it a few times before getting the right fit.

Once she did though, it was worth every bit of stress. Her breasts were cradled and pushed up, prominently displayed. The cups of the corset were cut low to expose her nipples and the front of her breasts. It was the most erotic thing she'd ever worn. Once she stepped into a pair of heels, her bottom was pushed up. When she looked again at her front view, the garter belt ran across her lower belly but left her entire pubic mound on display.

It was sexy and naughty. The candlelight added to its allure. She brushed her hair out and left it flowing freely to brush her shoulders.

Her clit started throbbing before she even opened the bathroom door.

The click of her heels against the tile seemed excessively loud. It wasn't the first time she'd planned to have sex, but it was so much more intense because she wasn't sure of Tarak. He was unpredictable, which accounted for the tremble in her fingers as she reached for the sliding door.

She gasped when she saw him. Tarak was stretched out along the foot of the bed, watching the bathroom door.

And the man was gloriously naked.

"That corset was worth all the trouble it took me to find it." His gaze was on her nipples—it looked like he wanted to lick them.

The candlelight flickered along his smooth skin, dancing over the hard ridges of his body. His cock stood out rock hard and perfect.

"Now, you are definitely worth waiting for… my pet."

Sabra swallowed and moved toward him, trying to move smoothly, confidently, but she felt stiff.

"Stop." He sat up, his expression tightening. Sabra paused, not really sure what to do. She wobbled just a tiny bit on her heels and ordered herself to find some poise.

It was an impossible task though, because Tarak was staring at her bared mons.

"I am going to lick that bare cleft."

It was what she'd hoped for, but hearing it out loud sent her heart racing. Without thinking, she started to cover her newly bared pubic region with her hands.

"Freeze." The order was clipped and short. "Put your hands behind your back, Sabra."

"Ummmm—"

There was a sudden snap of leather. She jumped, her eyes going wide as she caught sight of a black leather flogger in his hand. He'd had it behind his body. He pulled it between his fingers as she tried to swallow the lump clogging her throat.

"I've had a few relationships over the years that included power exchange moments, but I honestly have to admit"—he pulled his fingers along the ends of the flogger before looking her dead in the eye—"you're the first woman I've ever wanted submission from."

It was a compliment. A savage one maybe, but the honesty was blazing in his eyes.

"I want more than a fuck, Sabra. I want the trust to let me drive you to the edge."

She nodded, her tongue stuck to the roof of her mouth. He shook his head and lowered his feet to the floor. The room suddenly shrank, the impulse to move back a step almost overwhelming her.

"The safe word, Sabra." He stood up, crowding her even more. "That's how you give trust and how I respect it."

"Gold."

One dark eyebrow rose. "Rather fitting."

He started to circle her, taking slow, even steps she couldn't hear. She turned her head to follow his progress behind her.

"Eyes forward. I want to look you over, my pet."

She looked forward, only to discover he'd draped a towel over the mirror behind the headboard. She felt his gaze on her bare bottom and felt her pussy growing wet.

"Feet apart."

She was already complying before she thought about it. The position gave her slit enough room to separate and she smelled the scent of her own arousal. He snapped the flogger again and she jumped, stumbling forward a few steps before regaining her balance.

He slid a hard arm around her waist, helping to steady her, but all it did was blow up her control completely. His skin was smooth and hot against hers. That hard cock of his was pressed against her lower back, making her pussy ache for it.

"The flogger is a toy, Sabra, and I grew out of toys long ago." She heard him drop the flogger onto the floor. "I much prefer my bare hands."

"So do I," she muttered breathlessly.

He clicked his tongue in reprimand and bit the side of her neck gently. "Pets don't give their opinions."

He rubbed one of her buttocks before lifting his hand and delivering a soft smack. It popped and sent a ripple of sensation through her. He rubbed the spot gently before closing his hand around her neck and tipping her head back onto his shoulder. When she complied, he shifted, allowing his cock between her thighs. Her mind went into meltdown, arousal biting into her so hard she whimpered.

He stroked her throat, using a gentle touch as he teased her earlobe with his lips. He thrust his cock through her slit, the level of her arousal clear by how wet she was.

"Close your feet and give me something to fuck."

She wanted to lean forward, but he held her head back against his shoulder. She shuddered but moved her feet together.

"Mmmmm... very well done."

He thrust against her, the hard length of his cock teasing her clit every time it slid past.

"You will not come," he ordered in a raspy tone. "You will feel my release and be pleasured by the knowledge that your flesh gave me satisfaction, Sabra."

"*Oh shit*," she cussed, not sure if she was turned on or repulsed by the idea. All she could feel was a burning hunger. "I don't know… I don't know if—"

His grip on her throat tightened just a fraction, stopping her.

"You trust me to know what I need to give you."

"Okay."

She was trembling, sweat beading on her forehead as anticipation tormented her.

"Close your eyes." He stroked the column of her throat. "You'll know I'm close when my nipples harden. Tell me when you feel them."

His voice was almost disembodied. It felt as if it were inside her head, the pair of them one being. He was thrusting against her, his knees slightly bent so that he could keep his cock between the top of her thighs. Knowing he was going to come made her jealous. Her clit was aching with need, but all he did was tease it with every thrust.

"Cross your ankles, Sabra." His breathing was hard. "Squeeze my dick tighter."

"*Asshole*." She couldn't help herself; the word came out of her frustration. But she crossed her feet and tightened her legs.

She was so turned on his cock was slick with the juices spilling from her body. She didn't think she'd ever been so aroused in her life. Her nipples were beading and she was trying to lower her body, in an effort to press against his cock, but he held her still with the arm around her waist.

"Do you feel them yet?"

She was so concentrated on her lower body it took a moment for her mind to grasp what he said. Little grunts were escaping from his lips as he pumped against her faster.

"Yes!" She shimmied her shoulders and gasped. "Oh hell yes… your nipples are hard, Tarak."

The knowledge was like a wave crashing into her. Raw power surged through her, filling her as he growled and his cock started to jerk between her thighs. She gasped and squeezed him so tight her muscles ached. She could feel him losing control while she pressed hard enough to ensure he lost it completely. He snarled savagely next to her ear, holding her throat in place as she heard his come hitting the floor.

She shimmied again, slowly moving her shoulders against his hard nipples and rubbing her bottom against his cock. "That was intense," she said

He licked the outside edge of her ear. "Thank you for offering your ass."

Her eyes opened wide, and she tried straightening her neck. "That wasn't what I meant."

He slid his hand around and gathered up her hair, holding it firmly in a fist as he bent her over.

"Put your hands on the bed."

With her ankles still crossed, it was an awkward position. She was off balance, unsure, and mentally absorbed with the idea of having him touch her back entrance. But she flattened her hands on the foot of the bed, the crushing satisfaction of the last encounter fueling her need to continue.

He bent down and mopped up the floor. Their gazes met and he sat down behind her on the floor.

"Spread your legs."

He was going to watch her pussy open. Her cheeks flamed red as he watched.

"You took a good long look at my cock when you came out

of the bathroom." He reached over and picked up the flogger and began tapping it against the floor with a lazy rhythm. "I want to see your pussy."

She uncrossed her ankles and opened her legs. He stopped her with the flogger, laying it against the ankle she'd moved. The leather made her shiver.

"Watch my face as you spread yourself wider." He tapped a spot on the wood floor.

She licked her lower lip and moved her foot. His gaze was centered on her slit, his eyes narrowing when she moved. There was no way to explain the rush of confidence that filled her in that moment. He could have spoken a hundred compliments, but none of them would have matched the pure honesty she saw in his eyes.

He liked what he saw, desired it.

He teased the inside of her thigh with the flogger, running it up from her knee and then down again. She was so excited her clit gave a sudden twist, almost bursting with a climax in response.

"What a perfect submissive position and yet…" He tantalized the inside of her other thigh with the flogger. "I feel like I'm the one being held captive."

He stood up, disappearing from her sight. It stoked the excitement bubbling inside her. When he came back into view, there was a black leather sheath covering his cock. It even had a bag that held his balls. Frustration tore through her and she started to straighten up, intent on pulling the thing off what she craved.

He smacked her bottom in response, one hard spank that sent her back into the position he'd put her in. Her mind had barely registered the pain before he rubbed it away.

"Your pussy is very tempting—possibly too much." He slid his hand across her belly, making her clit pulse. "I have my limits, so a little deterrent is in order. We won't fuck until I take it off."

That was going to drive her crazy.

"Sit on the edge of the bed."

She straightened, realizing that her back was getting a little stiff. He'd pulled his desk chair in from the office and sat watching her as if she was performing on a stage. The black leather covering his cock matched the chair. It was a ridiculous little scrap, but it seemed to give him more shielding, more protection from her gaze than she had.

The power shifts were intoxicating.

She sat down and her shoes fell off because it was so high off the floor.

"A little further back."

She complied and found the seconds swelling up into little moments of eternity.

"Bring your legs up onto the bed. Spread them as wide as you can."

Being bent over had felt submissive, but she found opening her legs far more vulnerable. He reached down and toyed with the end of the leather sheathing his cock.

"Lie back, Sabra. Lie all the way back and keep your tender parts open for my pleasure."

Excitement twisted in her belly as she surrendered. Her senses were so heightened she heard his feet flattening against the wood floor. She felt him closing the gap, coming closer, nearer until the heat from his body reached out to touch hers.

"I'm... on the edge... Tarak!"

He stroked her belly, making her clit throb painfully.

"Look at me."

His voice was solid and full of control. She hissed because it wasn't fair. But she was helpless, the need to gain release driving her mad. He slid his hand down to the top of her recently bared mons.

"Come."

It was a short command, hard and demanding. He slid his finger between the folds of her slit and rubbed her clit. She convulsed, her entire body bucking as all the boiling need released in one hard burst of pleasure. She cried out, unable to control anything. She was at the mercy of the moment, his mercy, and in the depths of his glittering eyes, she could see that he knew it.

But she had given him that power.

It was balm for the heat rash covering her in the aftermath of that explosive moment. She felt she now had some sort of deeper understanding of her own effect on him. She'd heard it talked about but there was no understanding until that moment.

She rolled over, curling up to hug herself. Tears eased from her eyes as she found herself stripped down to her core. None of the ideas of who she thought she wanted to be remained, there was only the blunt reality of her personality.

And his.

The bed moved as he joined her, pulling her close as he kissed the tracks the tears left behind. She reached for him, eager to embrace the only man who seemed to understand her.

She caught his hair and used the grip to turn his head so she could kiss him. It was a hungry meeting of mouths, their lips stroking and slipping along one another before their tongues dueled. She reached down and grabbed the leather sheath and sent it flying across the room.

"I want you now," she demanded and pushed him onto his back. She climbed on top of him, sinking down onto his cock with a soft snarl of victory.

He reached up and cupped her breasts, kneading them as he bucked beneath her. "I might just throw you."

She braced her hands on his shoulders and clamped him between her thighs to hold tight. "Just try it."

He rose to her challenge, thrusting up, every time she plunged down. The bed shook and the headboard banged against the wall but she just went faster and harder. She looked down at his nipples and saw them tightening.

"You're coming with me, Sabra. I swear you are."

He tossed her onto her back and followed her, threading his fingers through hers and holding her hands against the mattress. She was his prisoner, and he started to hammer her hard. The change in position pressed against her clit harder. The bed rocked back and forth with his strength, the hard pace driving her desire to a fevered pitch. He ground his teeth together, holding back his pleasure until she screamed with another burst of release.

This one was deeper, rolling through her insides and centering around his hard flesh. She heard him growl as his cock jerked inside her. The hot spurt of his come pumped into her as he fucked her through the waves of climax.

He rolled onto the bed beside her and lay panting just as she did. Every muscle was useless, her body just a shattered shell.

"I've never enjoyed a power point meeting… quite so much." He slid an arm under her waist and pulled her against him. He nuzzled against her temple and kissed her forehead. "I think I need to choose my own safe word. Next time."

She smiled because she was too exhausted to laugh. More importantly, she was too satisfied to think about anything else.

So she didn't.

Chapter 9

"When are you going to see the second doctor, Dad?"

Her father was taking a long time answering. Sabra took a sip of her morning tea.

"I'm not going away, Dad. We had a deal."

"The secretary said they'd call me back," her dad replied at last.

"Don't you dare wait," Sabra insisted. "Give me the number."

"I'm a big boy, Sabra. I'll handle it."

Her dad had adopted the parental tone of no argument. She tapped her foot against the floor as she battled the urge to do it anyway.

"I love you, Dad."

"Ouch," her father remarked. "All right, I'll give them another call." She smiled. "Thanks, Daddy."

The line went dead and she finished her tea.

"What's wrong with your father?"

Tarak emerged from the bedroom dressed for the day.

"We're not sure," she answered as they went to the entry room for their boots. They had fallen into a pattern, and it was scary how comfortable it felt. Days were passing, and she was settling in deeper and deeper.

Now he was interested in her family. That sent two tears into her eyes.

Pansy.

"So tell me what you think it is," Tarak insisted.

Sabra knotted her bootlace. "It's his heart, but Dad is being very secretive about it."

"And that's worrying you."

She stood up and grabbed her coat. "Yeah. My dad always wants to take care of me. If he needs surgery, I'm going to need to fly home. I won't let him be alone."

She wasn't sure what he'd make of that, but she found him nodding as he opened the door for her.

"You have a sincere heart, Sabra." He followed her down the front steps but caught her wrist and pulled her back before she opened the door of the Terrain Tank Kurt was driving. "It scares me."

He cupped her jaw, the hold gentle yet so sincere that she shook. His eyes were clouded with indecision, something she wasn't used to seeing in him.

She reached for him, but he caught her hand and pressed a kiss against her fingertips. He was trying to control their relationship, just the way he managed Nektosha.

"In this case, I hope you don't succeed in controlling every detail of your life."

His eyes narrowed.

"Because I'm not looking forward to being alone in this relationship."

He released her hand and cupped her jaw. "I know you aren't, but you might have to settle for what I can give, Sabra." He reached past her and opened the door. "I'm afraid it isn't going to be as much as you have to offer."

~~~

The office was empty again. The test track was in full operation. The poor cook looked bored to tears, so Sabra told him to go down to the test track too. He offered her a bright smile before telling her there was a sandwich in the refrigerator for her lunch.

Sabra sighed with relief.

She didn't need a witness today. Her emotions were raw and too on display. Falling for Tarak was hard enough; fearing that he wasn't capable of reciprocating was terrifying.

She dove into her work and tried to keep her personal life locked behind a door of determination.

She jumped when her cell phone chimed with an incoming text message.

Now you're the one late for supper.

She stared at the message and grinned like an idiot. She suddenly felt all warm and gooey inside. Where there had been no hope that morning, she suddenly saw a forest of possibilities.

On my way, she texted back.

With a happy little bounce to her step, she grabbed her purse and jacket and headed out. Kurt wasn't in his office, but the cabin wasn't that far a walk. Besides, she'd been neglecting her workouts in favor of spending time in bed with Tarak. Not that she was complaining, but she would be if her butt doubled in size.

Besides, she felt drawn to the cabin. Tarak's last words shook her to her core but his text message gave her a jolt of hope. Waiting around was impossible, so she set off at a brisk pace. The daylight hours were still short. In a few months, they'd have sunlight eighteen hours a day, but they paid for it now with only six hours of light.

The wind had picked up, and she shivered as it blew snow at her back. Sabra pulled her hood up to keep it from getting inside her jacket, but her nose felt as though it were freezing. Ahead she could see the lights of the cabin and headed for them. She rubbed her hands and tried to warm up her face but only succeeded in chilling her fingers. Somewhere she had gloves. She patted her pockets and found a lump. She stopped to push her fingers into them. A shiver shook her and another one as she realized she was kicking snow with every step.

Funny, she recalled most of the snow being gone.

Well, it wasn't that big of a deal. It was light and powdery. But it started to melt against the top of her boots and her socks wicked the frigid water down to her ankles. Soon her toes were numb.

When she looked up, the lights were gone. Or maybe not. The air looked as though it were full of blowing feathers. It was magical really, and she stared at it for a long moment, just enjoying seeing actual snow fall—even if it was going at a sideways angle.

She shivered with the cold, but it fit the moment. In fact, she enjoyed being part of the snowstorm. She pulled her hands out of her pockets and let the feathers collect in her hands. It was so much softer than she'd imagined anything frozen might be. The wind blew her forward and she let it, loving the sensation of floating. When she stumbled and fell, she laughed as the snow flew up around her like a cloud.

She laughed at it and herself.

The sun suddenly came out, shining brightly against the shower of frozen droplets. She could see each one so clearly as the light increased until it was blinding her.

"Sabra!"

Her name was a jolt. It shattered the mesmerizing grip the storm had on her but left her disoriented. She looked around, trying to decide where she was and why her ears were buzzing.

Someone caught her shoulders. "Sabra? Goddamn it, what are you doing walking?"

Tarak's face came into view as he got close enough for the snow not to get between them.

"I was… just…" Her teeth chattered violently and she realized she couldn't move her fingers.

Tarak scooped her up and carried her into the sunlight. But

as they passed it, she realized it was the Terrain Tank's headlights. Someone opened the door, and Tarak tossed her up into the seat.

It really didn't matter all that much. She was sleepy and let her eyes close.

"Wake up, Sabra," Tarak insisted as he patted her cheek.

"Why?"

"Because you're slipping into hypothermia." He grabbed her hands and stuck them against his belly.

She stiffened, sucking in her breath at the startling contrast between his skin and hers. It was so dramatic it felt like a thousand pinpricks all over her palms.

"People die in this sort of weather."

"It's just… a… little… snow," she argued.

Someone was driving the Terrain Tank, and Tarak reached out to slip a hand behind her back as they bounced along the road.

"Your nose is like ice," he growled.

"Sorry." She tried to push herself away from him, but he cupped her head and pulled her close again.

Now her face was on fire. It stung as if she had scraped it up in a fall or something. The skin felt raw.

"I'm the one who's sorry, Sabra. I should have explained a few survival rules." He rubbed the back of her head. "I forgot you don't know a thing about snow."

She knew it could hurt now. Her entire body was shaking and all the exposed skin was burning, and no matter how hard she tried, she couldn't clench her jaw tight enough to stop her teeth from chattering.

"I was just walking… to the… cabin."

"You were heading back to the office when I used the location chip in your phone to find you."

"Oh… shit."

"Exactly."

The Terrain Tank stopped and someone opened the door. Tarak jumped down and reached up to pull her out of the seat.

"We need to get you out of these wet clothes."

He didn't stop in the coatroom but carried her all the way across the floor to the master bathroom. She looked over his shoulder at the snow he left behind on the wood floor.

"Tarak... the wood floor..."

"I don't give a shit about the floor, Sabra." He sat her on the edge of the Jacuzzi tub and turned the faucet on full blast. Steam started rising from the water and he took a moment to adjust the temperature. "I'm more concerned with your toes, angel."

She looked down and gasped. Her boots were packed with snow. She couldn't even see the laces. She reached down, but the moment she moved her fingers, pain raced through her hands.

She pulled them back toward her chest out of reflex. Tarak took a moment to inspect each hand before turning his attention to her boots.

"I think you've managed to escape frostbite on your hands. They are going to hurt like hell though."

He pulled a wicked-looking knife off his belt and used it to slice through the frozen laces. With a hard tug, her boot came free and Tarak tossed it across the bathroom floor.

"I don't understand... It didn't look like the weather was that bad."

"The night can hide a lot of things up here." He had her other boot off and began peeling her socks off. They were full of ice that crackled. "Some of those things are deadly if you don't know what you're doing. I should have trained you."

"I should have done some research."

He helped her stand and began to strip her. She tried to help, but her hands refused to work. It just hurt too much. Her lips felt as if they were sunburned, and she licked them.

Her clothing ended up scattered all over the floor. Tarak was like a bear, tearing away at the layers she had on without a care for the things he was ripping. He gave a satisfied grunt when she was bare.

She sat back down. He took a moment to strip before stepping over the side of the tub and into the water.

"This isn't going to be a bath you enjoy, Sabra." His voice was rough, but his touch was gentle. He scooped her up and cradled her against his chest before sitting down.

The water felt as if it were boiling her alive. She jerked, kicking water all over the place before she mastered the impulse.

"Sorry…" She gasped and clenched her teeth.

"Cuss all you want."

He settled her in the tub, holding her beneath the water as she fought back tears. She ended up with her head on his chest, shaking it back and forth.

"I don't want to cuss… at you. I was so happy when you sent me that text… I just wanted to get here and Kurt wasn't in his office."

"He was on the test track." Tarak smoothed a hand down her back. "I should have given you a truck to drive."

Someone pounded on the door.

"That will be Dr. Farr."

She lifted her head and locked stares with him as the sound of the door opening hit her ears.

"I'm naked."

"He's a doctor."

She struggled to get up. "I don't care."

Tarak growled at her. "You've never acted shy before."

She slipped as she tried to stand up. "With you, I'm just different."

He snarled something in Apache that sounded as though it were profane. He stood and helped to steady her. "Hold on, Farr. She wants to put something on."

"Copy that."

Sabra felt a blush coming on as the other man responded from just outside the bathroom door. The heat made her skin sting though, and she cussed softly.

But at least her hands were working. They smarted, but she succeeded in grabbing a towel and wrapping it around herself. Tarak disappeared inside the closet and returned with a fluffy bathrobe.

The look in his eyes when he knotted the tie around her waist was one she knew was going to haunt her. Self-recrimination was eating him alive. She reached out for him, but he shook his head.

"Doctor first."

He grabbed the towel and tucked it around his waist.

"Promise me."

He ignored her.

"Tarak, promise me we'll discuss this."

He picked her up and carried her into the bedroom, leaving her with the fact that he'd promised her nothing.

———

Tarak poured himself a drink but didn't touch it until the doctor came out of the bedroom. He was still zipping up his medical backpack.

"She's used her share of luck for the month," he offered as he got closer. "I gave her something for the pain. Call me if she develops any sort of cough or changes in skin color."

"Thank you."

The doctor gave him a salute before going into the coatroom to put on his outerwear. The storm was howling outside the windows, but the doctor was only going across the testing field to his rooms behind the Nektosha medical facility.

The outer door opened and closed, and Tarak reached for his drink.

———

"Put it down, Tarak."

He jerked around, fumbling the glass onto the counter.

"You need to be in bed."

She shook her head. "Not until you and I get one thing straight. This was not your fault." She made it to one of the chairs and sat down.

"It's not open for discussion, Sabra." He reached for the glass and took a large drink. "I made a decision that had consequences for you—serious ones."

"You bet I took it seriously when you said you cared about me."

His eyebrows lowered. "That's not the topic."

She smiled at him, but it was more of a promise than an expression. "This isn't an office. I don't have to stick to the meeting agenda."

"It's my home, so my rules."

Sabra lifted one hand and pointed at him. "It's only a home if you let someone share it with you, Tarak. Otherwise, it's the cabin you built to make your ex-fiancée jealous."

"I can live with that." He downed the last of his drink. "Because it beats the hell out of living with the fact that I let you walk into a snowstorm that could have killed you."

He'd stomped over to her, towering over her as he shook his head, rejecting every argument she made. It slashed at her fragile emotions, tearing through the happiness that had sent her walking because she was just so eager to be near him.

"Well, I can't."

She stood up and reached for him. Surprise flickered in his eyes, but she got her arms around his neck and pressed her lips to his before he reacted.

Or maybe he was reacting, because he shuddered, his large body quivering beneath her hands. She kissed him, but only for a moment before he caught a handful of her hair and took command.

His mouth took hers with a demand that was searing. Hungry

and ravenous, he pressed her for a deeper taste. A soft moan escaped from her. The kiss wasn't enough. She needed more, more of him.

He'd put some jeans on and she reached for the waistband.

"Sabra…"

"Shut up," she snarled as she hooked her fingers around his pants and pulled the top two buttons loose. "Why is this the only time you aren't in a hurry to fuck me? I want you naked, Tarak. *Now*."

His nostrils flared. The savage little detail captured her attention, mesmerizing her. She yanked the tie on her bathrobe open and shrugged the garment off her shoulders. Her heart was racing, the need to wrap her thighs around him consuming her.

His gaze lowered to her breasts.

"I love your tits, Sabra." He reached out and cupped them. They felt tight, as if they were swollen. She arched back, bracing her hands on the tabletop as he massaged them and closed his thumb and forefinger around her puckered nipples. "I love the way they bounce when I'm fucking you."

He pinched her nipples, sending a jolt of need straight down her spine to her clit. She gasped, the hunger gnawing at her insides. It was a raging need, only this time she didn't worry about the intensity of it; instead she welcomed it.

"Can you smell me, Tarak?" She lifted her butt onto the edge of the table and let her thighs separate.

He closed his eyes and drew in a deep breath. He rolled her nipples and made her wait for what felt like an eternity.

"Yeah, baby, I can smell your musk." He opened his eyes and let her see the wild need burning in them. "It's intoxicating." He backed up a step and tore his fly completely open. His cock sprang into sight, thick and hard and beautiful. "Do you like what you see, Sabra?" He stroked his cock, teasing her.

Tormenting her.

She didn't care how he took her, only that he did.

"I'll like it better when you give it to me."

Something crossed his face that hit her in the heart. It was a need deeper than the one coursing through her flesh.

"*It's yours,*" he rasped.

The table shuddered when he covered her, moving between her thighs with a lightning-fast motion. She purred softly as he penetrated, pressing deep inside her with one fluid thrust. It was perfection and torment too, his cock stretching her, filling her but falling short of satisfying her. She bucked, lifting her hips and straining toward him. She wrapped her hands around his shoulders, but he pressed her flat onto the table.

"I'm going to watch them bounce, Sabra."

It was a demand that filled her with excitement. He gripped her hips and held them firmly in place as he began to thrust.

To fuck.

She didn't shy away from the word. No, it was what she craved, the hard pounding of his flesh into hers. She arched and struggled to meet each plunge, clawing at the wooden top of the table as each thrust drove her closer and closer to the point of orgasm.

Sinking her teeth into her lips, she held back the sounds of pleasure. He leaned down, covering her with his body and pulled her chin down.

"Let me hear you come."

His eyes glittered with demand as he continued to thrust into her, and he held her down and captured her wrists too.

It was the final straw, the last bit that she needed to tumble over the edge into climax. She wrapped her legs around his lean hips, a single act of aggression to match against the hold he had on her. She lifted herself up, pressing against him as the pleasure crested and crashed through her.

"Your nipples are hard little spikes against my chest, Sabra." His tone was dark and almost hypnotic. "And the sounds you make when I'm inside you drive me insane."

He kissed the side of her neck, sending a soft ripple of delight down her body before straightening up. He renewed his grip on her hips and pulled her toward him as he hammered his way to climax. It was savage and mesmerizing to watch. The lights were still on, giving her a clear view of the raw enjoyment tightening his features. He curled his lips back as he drove his cock faster and harder into her sex.

She felt his penis jerk as he let out a groan. She tightened her legs around him, pulling him tight against her as he rode out the orgasm. He growled and his cock jerked inside her. He ended up leaning on the table, his chest laboring to draw in enough breath. They were both coated in perspiration while the snowstorm ragged outside the windows.

"I love the way you make your points, Sabra."

He scooped her up and carried her to the bedroom. Across from the bed was a huge flat-screen television. Once they were snuggled down beneath the covers, he flipped it on.

"Any requests?"

She rubbed a hand across his chest, idly toying with the crisp hair. "Something with springtime."

"Like *Bambi*?" he offered mockingly.

She shook her head. "No. Bambi's mommy gets killed."

He opened up a menu of movies and started at the top of the alphabet. "*Alien*?"

"Everyone gets killed in that one." She gently slapped his shoulder. "You need practice at date night."

"Not according to those moans you let out when you came hard enough to milk my dick."

"I knew you were arrogant the first time I saw you."

He settled on a comedy and hit the play button.

"I had no idea how much trouble you were going to be." He wrapped his arms around her and kissed the top of her head. "Have

I told you how much I like surprises? It takes a lot to show me something more than I was expecting."

It was a simple word that settled into her heart. Maybe it was the brush with death, but she suddenly needed more than affection. The reason was clear. The man had stolen her heart. It shouldn't have been so simple, shouldn't have happened so fast, but there was no denying it. She fell asleep knowing she was completely at his mercy.

Chapter 10

"THIS LIST IS A mile long," Sabra groused.

Tarak didn't even blink in response. Sabra felt her frustration boiling when she took a second look at the survival training list he'd put together for her. Her attention settled on one in particular.

"I am not going to 'clean and gut' anything, much less a bunny," she informed him.

He smacked his lips. "Bunny rabbit is good eating."

"Don't be a bully."

He looked into the open backpack sitting on the kitchen counter and surveyed the contents. He zipped it up a moment later and shrugged it over one shoulder.

"I'm being a caring, concerned boyfriend who is going to make sure you can handle anything this frontier land tosses at you."

"Ha!" she barked on the way to the coatroom to put her boots on. "You're laughing at me behind that poker face."

"That's part of the fun, I hear." He finished tying his boots and opened the outer door. "I'm a little rusty at the whole courtship thing."

"Is that why we skipped to the sex?"

He slapped her bottom as she passed by him. "Stop trying to distract the instructor."

"A moment ago you were my boyfriend," she complained and propped a hand on her hip. "Now you're saying I screwed the teacher."

"Way better than bringing me an apple."

She choked as she climbed into the Terrain Tank. "I guess I know how to tell you I'm pissed at you—one large apple."

He spared a sidelong glance at her. "I'll gag you with it while I spank you."

Heat teased her cheeks. A crazy little twist of excitement went through her clit too. After that one wild fuck, their sex life had been remarkably tame since her brush with hypothermia. Tarak handled her carefully and tenderly. It left her feeling as if something were getting ready to snap.

When he'd handed her a list, she wasn't sure if it was a Dear Jane letter or not. Her heart had been pounding so hard, she'd had to wipe sweat off her forehead.

Let him think it was the bunny rabbit that had her sweating. It was better than admitting she was afraid he'd done exactly what he'd wanted to do—fucked her out of his system.

He certainly wasn't out of hers. If anything, the last week of soft kisses and nighttime cuddles had left her further involved with him. Her emotions were stronger and harder to reason out. Logic wasn't prevailing anymore.

"Okay, first lesson: rifle loading."

She got out of the Terrain Tank and gasped at the view. He'd driven up the hillside that enclosed the test facility like a huge cauldron. At the top of the ridge, they could see for miles and miles of untamed wilderness. The snow had melted away again, leaving only a few wet patches under the shade of the trees. The sky was immense and bluer than she could ever recall southern California's being. The air was crisp and smelled like pine.

"It's amazing up here." She drew in a deep breath and let it loose with a happy little sigh. When she opened her eyes, she found Tarak staring at her.

"What?"

He shook his head, denying her his feelings.

"Don't you think some people actually like the great outdoors?"

He stopped fiddling with the rifle and locked gazes with her. "I haven't met too many females who do."

"If Anastasia is an example of the type you go for, I can understand."

He pulled the firing pin back on the rifle to check its action. "Lately, you're my type." He pointed the gun down the hillside. "But if you're going to be staying into spring, you need to know how to handle a gun. We get moose, caribou, bears—and that includes grizzlies." He handed her the rifle.

"It's been a few years, but my dad used to take me camping."

He gave her a doubting look.

"Loading first."

He opened a box of ammunition that was sitting on the bumper of the Terrain Tank, and she reached for a bullet. It was larger than anything her dad had ever taught her to fire, but the concept was still the same.

Yeah right. She'd been with guys before, but Tarak was in a whole other category as far as men went.

The concept was so not the same, at least not when it came to Tarak.

She didn't just want to have fun. The need to impress him was burning inside her. She wanted to be worthy, which sounded a little too submissive, but she couldn't very well lie to herself. The need was there, just like all the other cravings Tarak unleashed in her. It felt as though she needed to prove herself.

She loaded the gun while he watched. His expression didn't give much away, but the bullet loaded into the chamber easily. She got the gun into the right position and figured out how to look down the sights. Tarak moved up behind her, using his hands to guide her as he looked down the barrel of the gun with her.

The scent of his skin mixed with the pine. It was more potent than any cologne. Tarak and the rugged landscape were a perfect combination.

"Now squeeze gently," he whispered next to her ear.

"I know how to handle your weapon, Tarak."

The gun went off. She purred softly as he steadied her.

"You need to make sure your stance is wide and open," he whispered against her ear, "or you might get tossed when it goes off."

"I'll do my best to hold tight."

He pressed up against her, the hard outline of his cock teasing her bottom. Her pussy was heating up and all she could do was think about how long the list that he'd given her was.

There was no satisfaction coming her way for a while, but at least it was a game two could play.

"Wide and open…" She wiggled her bottom against his cock. "Got it."

"Not yet you don't." He adjusted the position of the rifle and thrust against her hips. "You want to clench those buns when you go for the shot."

The gun went off again before he let her lower it.

He pressed a warm kiss against her neck before moving back to the Terrain Tank to retrieve the backpack. "Let's take a hike."

They left the vehicle behind and climbed through the forest. He handed her a compass and she laughed.

"This looks like one my dad used to have."

"High-tech isn't always the best method out here. That doesn't have a battery to go dead." He watched her open it up. "There's a lake southeast of here."

"Where's the topography map?"

His poker face broke and he opened a pocket on his vest. "That's one gold star."

He handed her the map. She studied it for a moment, checking the elevation lines before deciding which way to go. Sometimes, a straight path would lead you to a cliff and you spent a lot of time backtracking.

"I like my stars with no wrinkles in them, so make sure you use the center of the sheet of tinfoil."

"Yeah, I know you like the center." His voice turned hungry. "Right down the center."

Her clit throbbed and her nipples tightened. "Sorry, I'm in class and you're distracting me."

She took off toward the lake, listening to Tarak chuckling behind her. The ground was soggy in places from the snowmelt. There were also white ribbons of water flowing down the hillsides that surrounded them. The sound of rushing water was like background music.

Tarak reached out and caught her shoulder at one point. He pointed up the slope. A brown bear was walking along the river, peering intently into the water. He jumped into the water but came out empty-handed.

"That's a brown bear," Tarak informed her. "Most of the time they'll leave you alone unless you have food. If you see one with a cub, stay away from it."

His warning wasn't really needed. She had no interest in getting too near anything that was so much larger than herself. Somehow, she couldn't recall her camping trips with her father including wild animals.

She picked up the pace, determined not to turn into a wimp.

The lake wasn't really very far. She heard the water before she saw it. Once they broke through the trees, she understood why. There was a large flow of water coming down the mountainside to feed into the lake. It was really more of a flooded valley, the water spilling off the far end where the elevation was lower.

Trees grew close to the edge, but there were also several large flat spots of exposed granite rock. The water looked cleaner than any she'd seen in her life. It seemed to make the very air smell good too.

"How are you going to feed me?"

She turned away from the lake and looked back to find Tarak sitting on a bare patch of rock.

"I've got two broken arms," he informed her.

"Is that a fact?"

He nodded, challenging her with his poker face.

"I guess I'd better see what's in the backpack." She marched over to where he'd dropped it and unzipped the main compartment.

"I forgot the fishing gear," he insisted.

"Hmmm, there's more than one way to catch a fish." She pulled a large trash bag from the backpack and a Leatherman tool. Pulling the scissors out of the Leatherman, she began to cut the trash bag along one side.

"Sure you want to use something that could be helpful in building a shelter? It rains a lot here."

"There are three more," she replied quickly. "And that outcropping of granite will make a good shelter."

She began to fold the plastic and cut it like a giant snowflake. By the time she was done, she'd made a crude sort of plastic net. The backpack also yielded an ax. She grabbed it, walked over to a pine tree, and hacked off two thin branches. Once she'd skinned the needles off, she used some duct tape to secure the long branches along the side of her net.

"Impressive," he commented.

"Only if I catch a fish."

But she was determined to succeed. Adrenaline was pumping through her system, keeping her warm as she took off her boots, rolled up her pants, and waded out into the current. She stuck the net into the water at an angle and waited. The water bubbled passed her ankles and an eagle screeched somewhere above her. It landed on the branch of a tree, watching her.

Eagles meant fish. She recalled a nature documentary she'd seen long ago where they'd showed bald eagles catching wild salmon.

Something pushed against the plastic and she lifted the two sides of her net up to trap it in the center. The fish struggled to escape, and she turned around, giddy with her accomplishment. The rocky bottom of the stream was slippery and her feet went shooting out from under her. She landed in the water, squealing as it soaked her.

But she kept her fish.

She stood up with a huff and trudged toward the shore. Tarak was on his feet, a suspicious pinched look to his lips.

"Don't laugh at she who catches you dinner."

She made her way to shore before opening the net to see what she'd caught. It was a fairly large fish, and she smiled with triumph.

"That was pretty good, Sabra." He pulled a knife from his belt and offered it to her handle first.

She shook her head. "We have to build the shelter and get a fire going before we gut the fish."

He nodded. "But now that you have it, the bears will be interested."

She narrowed her eyes. "My teacher seems to like the 'learning on the job' approach or he might have mentioned that."

He stuck the knife back into his waist scabbard and picked up the fish by the tail. "I'll get the fire going."

"Those arms healed mighty fast. Kind of a pity."

He'd already started toward the outcropping and turned to look back at her. She offered him a wicked look. "I could think of a few things to do with you that might be fun if you didn't have the use of your arms."

He smiled slowly and very deliberately flipped her the bird.

"Sorry, I have to catch more fish, so that's not going to happen."

He laughed at her, the sound following her as she went back to fishing. The sun dried her shirt and the back of her jeans, but she was still damp when she caught the third fish.

Tarak had a fire set up, but it looked as if he was waiting for her to light it. She climbed out of the water and made her way over to him. Once more, he had his poker face on and was waiting to see what she'd do. He'd gathered a pile of wood and she searched among it for tinder. Once she had a handful of soft, dry bark, she put it under the tepee of wood and pulled a flint striking tool out of the survival knife that had been in the backpack.

"Not bad, Sabra, not bad at all."

She smiled, enjoying the praise. Okay, she was also enjoying the fact that she wasn't failing at his challenge. That gave her a different sort of feeling, something that was deeper and far more precious. She felt like she could match him. It was confidence, not arrogance, and she realized she'd mistaken it a few times on him. The man had his share of arrogance, that was for sure, but a lot of it he'd earned. Only an idiot would get mad about it.

The world was full of those too, people who critiqued and criticized those who had earned what they themselves wanted. Sure, you could make derogatory remarks about a male model, but the bottom line was, no one could buy a muscular frame. It took discipline and commitment.

Tarak had Nektosha because he'd stuck it out in the wilderness and still drove himself night and day.

"You're lost in thought, Sabra."

She looked up. "Guilty." The wood was popping as it caught fire. "My dad used to tell me that going out into the woods was a way to clear your thoughts, but you needed to close your mouth for it to happen."

He laid the cleaned fish parts over a few pieces of wood to begin cooking. There was the sound of a zipper opening as he rummaged around in the backpack and came up with some salt and pepper.

"So this is a top-of-the-line roughing-it trip."

He sprinkled some of the pepper on the fish and then used the salt. "Anything tastes good when you're hungry, but a little salt can really make it great."

"I'm enjoying this trip. It's really fulfilling my need for something more." He stared at the cooking fish, but she knew he'd heard her. She wasn't going to be sorry that she'd said it. "If that makes you uncomfortable, too bad."

He turned to look at her but she wasn't finished. "I spent two years in a relationship with Kevin, too worried about making him feel chained to say what was on my mind. I'm not going that route again. If that means I'm fast-tracking us to a fiery ending, I guess I am."

"Do you challenge me like that because you know I find it irresistible? Pushing into my comfort zone to see if I'll push back, Sabra? It's a dangerous game. I'm not completely sure how I'll respond," he warned.

She choked on a bark of amusement, the sarcastic sort. "I know, but everything about our relationship is extreme. We're not camping; we're surviving in the Alaskan wilderness. Even the moment I met you was an extreme one. It makes controlling what I say too hard. But that's really just an excuse. I don't want to play some stupid game of making sure I don't bruise your spirit of bachelor freedom—or whatever it's called when guys think they're the only ones who feel cornered."

He cupped her chin, his hand warm and strong. It was like some sort of electrical connection between them. Her insides started twisting the second he touched her.

"Something about you makes me want to corner you, Sabra." His eyes flashed with hunger. "It's dark and damn near uncontrollable."

He pressed his lips against hers. She opened her mouth and kissed him back. He captured her, slipping his arms around her and pulling her into his lap. It gave her the opportunity to stroke his neck and push her fingers into his hair. She ran her tongue across his lower lip, teasing him as she straddled him.

He growled at her, cupping the back of her head and twisting her hair in his fist. The kiss became harder, more demanding as he pressed her mouth open and thrust his tongue inside.

She felt invaded, but it unleashed a wave of excitement that washed all the way through her. There wasn't a part of her body that didn't feel it. It left her twisting with anticipation, her clit pulsing with need. He reached down and boldly rubbed her sex.

She jumped, startled by the jolt of sensation that went through her.

"I think we need to get you out of those wet clothes, Sabra."

"The clothes aren't what's wet."

He yanked his jacket off and spread it over the rock. "I know."

There was a dark promise in his tone that made her fingers tremble as she began to strip. She got her boots off, but she looked around before lifting her top.

"There's no one around and I don't care if I'm wrong." He stood up and opened her jeans. He stripped them and her underwear down her legs and scooped her up before she realized what he was doing. He settled her on the jacket, pushing her thighs wide.

"The perfect appetizer."

His breath hit her wet slit. It was almost too much of a contrast. She jerked, unable to control her actions. He pressed her down, his shoulders keeping her thighs spread.

"I've never wanted to eat a woman out as much as I do you." He looked up her body, his eyes glittering with hard purpose. "I think it's a control issue, but you know something, Sabra? I like it."

He stroked her slit with one fingertip. Sensation coursed through her, but he had her pressed down, controlled.

And he liked it; she could see that in his dark eyes.

"You're not sure you're comfortable with it either," he continued as he ran his fingertip along the outside edge of her slit. The skin was ultrasensitive, kindling a need to have him make his way to more needy places.

"But I do, and I'm going to make sure you love it." He drew his fingertip straight down the center of her slit. "In the end."

Her eyes fluttered closed. It was a last-ditch defense against the vulnerable position he had her in. But her legs spread open easily, shamelessly really. While her pride might protest being spread out in front of a man who was still clothed and dignified, her body was quivering with anticipation.

He toyed with her first, his experience showing through as he stroked the tops of her thighs, running his hands along them and then returning to her knees to stroke her inner thighs.

"Making you come is like an aphrodisiac, and I honestly didn't believe in such things before meeting you, Sabra."

He leaned forward, teasing her slit with his warm breath, making her stomach muscles strain as she waited for the first lick.

"But the scent of your arousal turns my thinking completely off. There's nothing left but the need to taste you."

"God, I hope so…" The words were torn from her in a raspy tone. She was responding to him, her body a boiling cauldron of need.

He licked her first. One slow swipe of his tongue through the center of her slit. She cried out, almost on the edge of orgasm.

"It's not going to be that simple, Sabra." He pressed his finger into her pussy, circling the entrance while she sucked in huge gasps of breath. "I'm not going to let you cut this short."

He thrust his finger deep inside her, granting her the motion she craved but not the fullness of his penis.

"As I said," his voice dipped low, "you challenge me."

She opened her eyes in time to see his attention lowering to her spread sex. It should have struck her as raunchy or lewd, but the sight only served to increase the anticipation tightening her core.

He stretched forward, closing his lips around her clit.

"Oh Christ!"

Her hips bucked, the need to climax becoming an obsession.

Even drawing breath paled in compassion. There was nothing but the steady pulling of his lips around her clit. Each suck pushed her closer to the edge. One thrust from his finger would send her over the edge into mindless pleasure, but he denied her that last need.

"Tarak... I need to come!" She strained toward his mouth, desperate for enough pressure to fulfill her hunger.

"You'll look at me when you do."

He thrust two fingers up inside her, working them with a firm motion that fed the burning hunger inside her. But without his mouth, her clit didn't have what it needed. He withheld that pressure until she opened her eyes and looked down her body at him again.

"Very good."

He was commanding her, dominating her, and her pride wanted to rage, but she was helpless, caught in the grip of need and her knowledge of how good it would feel when he fed her cravings. He was the only one who drove her to such heights and she knew it, couldn't argue against it.

"Make me come, Tarak."

She cast the gauntlet down, baring her teeth as she did it. She wanted more than satisfaction from him; she wanted to be taken.

He showed her his teeth, curling his lips back to growl at her.

"Give me your cream, Sabra."

He massaged her clit again, sucking hard and pumping his fingers in and out of her sheath. She couldn't keep her eyes open. It was as if her brain simply couldn't deal with visual input because it was so overwhelmed by what was happening to her lower body.

She let out a thready, hoarse cry. Her spine felt like it might crack as she arched, every muscle so tight it was at snapping point. She was at her limit, pushed to the boundary of sanity and control. Once it all broke, she was tossed into a vortex of pleasure that tumbled her over and over like a stone until every edge was worn smooth.

"That was perfect."

His voice was full of victory while she felt like a boneless heap. Satisfaction was glowing inside her, but he was still working his fingers in and out of her. It was a soft stroking that completed the moment. Her clit was too sensitive to be touched, but he seemed to know it.

He knew too damned much about her.

It was a frustrating thing because it made her feel off balance and exposed.

But he stood up and stripped, his motions hard and jerky. His cock was swollen and red. "I want to hear that again."

She licked her dry lips, shivering as he lowered himself over her. "I won't come again... so soon."

His lips curved with determination. "Yes you will."

The first orgasm had left her sopping wet. He groaned as he pressed his length into her. He felt larger, harder than she recalled, the walls of her pussy stretching to accommodate him.

"I'm going to fuck you until you scream, Sabra."

He pushed her shirt up and lifted her breasts out of the cups of her bra.

"Perfect," he announced as he placed her thighs over his shoulders and thrust deep. Her breasts jiggled with the motion, gaining a low sound of enjoyment from him. But he lingered inside her, his eyes narrowing to slits as he remained still.

"You're so damned tight."

He pulled free, opening his eyes wide to lock gazes with her before thrusting smoothly into her again. He was possessing her, making sure she knew he was setting the pace. He wasn't content with just thrusting; he pressed against her, making sure he was balls deep inside her before pulling out for the next plunge.

"You're the first woman I've ever needed to dominate."

She could see the frustration in his eyes, feel it in the way he was holding back his urges. It was almost tangible, the tension making everything that much more intense.

"You're the only man I've ever submitted to." She stretched her legs out and folded her legs so she could hook her hands around her knees. The position spread her slit wide and kept her from having any range of motion. She was simply his, ready for possession.

"Hell yes!"

He gazed on her like a hungry predator. There was a savage delight flickering in his eyes as he fucked her. His face grew tight, the muscles along his neck cording as he kept the pace slow. It was building a hunger in her again, the slow, hard thrusts awakening her clit.

Her legs began to shake, the effort of remaining still taxing her. They were both covered in sweat, their breathing harsh.

"Give it up to me, Sabra."

The sun had faded completely, leaving him lit only by firelight in a primitive red and orange glow. The flames danced across his skin with a hypnotic effect. He increased his pace, sending another orgasm rolling through her. This time it was slow and deep, a moan of pure rapture escaping through her clenched teeth.

"That's right…" He pounded against her, a sound of savage satisfaction coming from him as his cock began to jerk inside her. He didn't fuck her through it but kept his length lodged inside her as the orgasm went through him. She tightened her vaginal muscles around him, squeezing as tight as she could.

"Sabra!" he gasped, and his cock delivered another spurt of hot come deep inside her. "Yes… *yes*!"

It felt as though her heart was going to burst. She lost her grip on him and her knees, every muscle she had, refused to move. She was a quivering mess, grateful for the rock beneath her.

Tarak fell forward, catching his weight just before he landed on top of her. He rolled over, ending up on the bare surface of the rock.

Time had no meaning as she caught her breath. It could have been five minutes or an hour; she had no idea.

Tarak finally rolled over and checked the fish. The moment he moved it, the scent teased her nose. The pepper gave it a spicy smell and her belly rumbled.

"Looks like we managed not to burn our dinner," he announced.

She sat up and reached for her jeans.

"Don't."

She looked back at him in confusion.

He stood up and offered her a hand. "Let's rinse off before it gets too cold." He'd set the fish on a rack further out from the fire to keep it warm. She took his hand and stood up.

He grabbed her shirt and pulled it over her head. She unhooked the closure of her bra and tossed it down on top of his jacket. He rummaged around in the backpack and pulled something out of it.

"Lightweight backpacking towel."

He hung it over his shoulder as he grasped her hand and led her down to the water. "Take my advice, just go in."

He really wasn't planning on letting her make up her own mind about it either. He trudged right into the water, pulling her behind him as she sputtered at the chill.

"Bastard!" she cursed him. "This is frickin' ice."

He pulled her deeper until her butt was covered. "No, it was ice about two days ago."

"Great. Thanks for letting me know I'm exaggerating."

He grinned and jumped backward. He landed with a huge splash, sending a wall of water at her. There was enough light coming off the moon to turn him into a silver god when he rose from the water.

"Try it, Sabra. My people used to use water for purification." He laid back and did a gentle stroke to keep himself afloat. "Right now I feel it working on me." He opened his eyes and pegged her with a gaze which was far more open than normal. "Do it with me."

Her legs no longer felt as if they were freezing. "All right." She jumped forward, swimming out until she was next to him. He captured her hand, his warm fingers encasing hers.

"Dive."

She held her breath and ducked beneath the surface of the water. It was freezing, but there was something completely soul refreshing about it. When she stood up again, she sighed. The hold on her hand was strong and anchoring. The water was running out of her hair and down her back. Tarak moved in front of her, the uncivilized picture he presented making her breathless.

"You look amazing, Tarak, like an echo from the last century."

He moved close enough for his heat to touch her. He cupped her face and kissed her. It was a slow meeting of their mouths, tender and something she longed to savor.

"You look like a myth I heard about but lost faith in finding on earth." He pulled her close and kissed her temple. "You feel like my soul mate."

She shivered, but it had nothing to do with the water temperature. Her heart was soaking up his words and letting something grow she knew she had no control over.

He drew in a deep breath and led her out of the water. She shivered as she used the towel to dry off and handed it to him.

The granite rock was smooth against her bare feet. She had an odd connection to the land around her as she walked stark naked across the open space to the fire, as if she'd been there before, in another life. It gave meaning to the intensity of her connection with Tarak, the words *soul mate* offering a strange logic to their relationship.

She had no idea what it meant—only that it felt incredible.

A cell phone buzzed while they were eating dinner.

She looked up from her rock plate as Tarak wiped his fingers on the towel and opened a pocket on his vest.

"That's wicked good reception."

"It's a satellite phone." He ran his fingertip across the screen and answered the call. "We're ready."

"Ready for what?" she asked.

He pushed the end call button and put the cell phone back in his pocket. "For some comfort."

A low rumble started in the distance. It sounded like a bee. It grew louder and louder until she could identify it as a helicopter. She turned and watched it hone in on them. It stopped just on the other side of the lake clearing, its rotors whipping up the surface of the water and making the trees dance. It lowered to touch down on the granite rock, but the rotors never stopped. Someone opened the side door and dropped two bundles. The man closed the door and the craft lifted off.

Tarak got up and went over to the bundles. Sabra followed him, curiosity chewing on her.

"You've been such a good little student, I thought you deserved some bedding." He tossed one of the bundles to her and it turned out to be a rolled up sleeping bag.

"Somehow, I don't think you're praising me for my survival skills."

He chuckled wickedly and pulled something from another bundle. "At least you can't accuse me of trying to soften your resolve with wine."

The moonlight washed over a bottle clenched in his hand.

"You're showing off."

Tarak shrugged. "Maybe a little. Are you impressed?"

"Only if it's chilled and it comes with dessert."

She carried the sleeping bag over to the shelter he'd built while she fished. All he'd done was lean branches against the rock face to give them a partial wall. A thick bed of fresh pine needles was piled up for their bed.

The sleeping bag was going to be a nice addition.

A really nice one.

He popped the cork on the wine bottle, and she turned around to watch him pouring it into two glasses.

"Is this a graduation celebration of Tarak Nektosha's survival course?"

"Yes."

She took the glass and smiled at the chill coming through the glass from the wine.

"Now that was precise timing."

He nodded and sipped his wine before setting it on the rock and opening a black case. Inside were chocolate-covered strawberries, a selection of cheeses, and petit fours.

Sabra took a strawberry and hummed when she bit into it.

"I can call them back if you want to sleep in a bed tonight."

His tone didn't give anything away, but she felt as though it were a test of some sort. Maybe it was a test of her own feelings.

"Call me selfish, but I like knowing your office phone isn't going to start ringing. Something tells me your clients don't have that satellite phone number."

"Nope," he answered before popping a petit four into his mouth. "If we stay here, I'm all yours."

"I like the sound of that." She lifted her wineglass for him to fill again.

They sat cross-legged on the rock, watching the fire. But two glasses of wine finished her off and she yawned.

"I'll roll out the bedding," Tarak informed her.

There was one drawback to the rustic location and that was the lack of a restroom. There wasn't even an outhouse, but she chided herself for worrying so much about it.

The sleeping bag was a double-wide one that covered the entire pine-needle bed. She untied her boots as Tarak disappeared into the woods. He returned and checked the rifle before propping it up next to the head of the bed. Two pillows were lying there, and he stacked them up before lying down and crooking a finger at her.

"Come here, Sabra. I'm going to enjoy my night off the grid."

She suddenly felt shy, like a girl on her first date. There was an intimacy present which she hadn't expected. She moved down and Tarak pulled her close.

The stars shone brilliantly. The side of the shelter he'd left open allowed them a full view of the nighttime sky. As she settled against him, she began to absorb the beauty on display. "This is neat."

"Are you serious?"

His question surprised her. "Yes. Any chance we'll see the northern lights? That's on my bucket list."

"We're not far enough north, but we could go up to Denali when it warms up. Mt. McKinley is spectacular when it comes out of the clouds."

"Cool." She drew in a deep breath and let it out. "Why do you doubt I'm serious?"

He rubbed her shoulder and pulled the sleeping bag up to cover her completely.

"I think I might have been testing you without admitting it to myself." His arms tightened around her for a moment. "I owe you an apology for that."

"Not really." She rubbed her hand along his chest, just enjoying the feeling of their warm skin meeting compared to the crisp night air. "This feels like a more sincere moment with you than a limo ride would. That would be a dead giveaway that all you wanted was sex."

It made sense in a funky sort of way. He wouldn't bother to test her if he didn't care.

"You understand me, Sabra, and I'm not sure how to handle it."

She yawned and smoothed her hand along the side of his jaw. "I love you and it scares the hell out of me."

He captured her hand and pressed a kiss against her wrist. Tears prickled her eyes, but she blinked them away because he'd feel them. The darkness was a curtain to help shield her pride. He was hiding within its folds too. It made it possible to confess, but it didn't make it any easier to hear nothing in return.

She'd just given him the power to destroy her. The hard part was trusting him enough not to use it.

※

Tarak's phone was ringing when they returned to the cabin the next evening. Sabra waved good-bye and blew him a kiss before heading off to the bathroom for a shower.

She heard him talking in the office on the opposite side of the master bedroom. He was still in there when she went to bed that night. She woke up to him nuzzling up against her, his hair still wet from the shower.

"My period showed up."

"Hmm?"

He lifted his head and looked down at her.

Sabra rubbed her eyes and tried to keep them open. "Just so you know there's nothing to stress about."

He kissed her shoulder and she went back to sleep. Monday morning arrived right on time, and they hurried off to the office with the rest of the crew.

But man, what a weekend.

Chapter 11

HER PERSONAL PHONE WENT off in the middle of the day. Sabra ignored it. A few minutes later someone stepped into her office without knocking. Tarak stormed straight to her desk.

"Why do you have to be the only one of my VPs who actually ignores their personal life during working hours?"

"Because my boss is a hard-ass," she retorted with dry humor. "But I like his tight ass."

His face grew dark but there was something in his eyes that made her abandon her teasing. It looked as if he were cornered.

"Okay, what's happening?"

He stepped back, looking as though the office were closing in on him. "Walk with me."

She hadn't made it around her desk when he was already through the doorway. Kurt looked up as Tarak crossed the main office hallway at a half sprint. He held his office door open for her and closed it with a thud once she was inside.

He ran a hand through his hair. "I'm going to ask you not to leave, Sabra."

He sounded tormented and it cut into her. When he turned his gaze on her, it was full of fear. The sight socked her in the gut.

"I'm not going anywhere."

"You don't understand," he interrupted her. He caught her biceps and pulled her close. "I gave you that damned ticket, and I'm asking you not to use it."

She reached out and cupped his jaw. He jerked, but his eyes closed and it looked as though he was savoring her touch, soaking it up because he feared it might be the last time he felt it.

"Tell me what the problem is, Tarak."

He opened his eyes. "Anastasia is on her way up here."

Sabra recoiled, but he held her close.

"Her father is a client, and he comes up to take a test drive once in a while, but I sure as hell didn't think she'd set foot up here. It's not her style."

She swallowed hard and laid her hands on his chest. "If you say she wasn't expected, I believe you."

Surprise registered on his face. "That simple?"

She smoothed her hands over his tight pectorals. "A relationship isn't much without trust."

He pulled her close, covering her lips with his. The kiss was hungry and seeking, their mouths meeting as though they were ravenous for a taste of each other. He bound her against his body, holding her as if he planned never to let her loose. But he did drag his head away.

"Security will keep an eye on her. I don't want her attacking you again."

The testing facility was a secured one. She'd seen the armed guards near the perimeter and around the hangars where the test vehicles were stored.

"I don't need protection."

He sat back and folded his arms across his chest.

"Ah hell," she groused. "You just adopted the boss position."

His lips curled. "So you know you're going to lose this argument."

"Fine. But I'm going to order a whole lot of DVDs tonight and start some self-study, since I can't get to my martial arts classes," she informed him. "I'm using your credit card too."

He smiled, the expression genuine. The phone on his desk started buzzing and he picked it up.

She walked back into the hallway and made it to her office before her façade crumbled. Her trust in his feelings was as thin as tissue. *I care about you* wasn't *I love you.*

And she loved him.

Without a doubt and so deeply, she suddenly understood how he had built an entire cabin out of the pain left from a broken heart.

"The test track is firing up." Kurt popped his head into her office in the afternoon. "Got some clients here. Are you coming?"

Sabra shook her head. Kurt came all the way into view, the excitement in his eyes turning to disappointment.

"Don't let that stop you, Kurt. I'm fine."

He stood undecided in the doorway. Sabra opened her desk drawer, pulled out a set of keys, and jingled them.

"It's clear as a summer day," she assured him. "I can get myself home."

Kurt's face lit up like a kid's on Christmas. "Give a call if you need anything."

He was off a moment later, hurrying to catch up with the rest of the office personnel. When the test track was open, they all found a reason to abandon their desks.

Well, she had a mighty good reason to avoid the test track.

Chicken.

On second thought, she wasn't going to be that hard on herself. There was something to be said for knowing how to pick your battles. Tarak was worth fighting for, but that victory would go to the woman who faced the man head on. Bickering with his ex-girlfriend wasn't going to impress him.

There was the distant roar of the test track again and it went on for the next few hours. At least with everyone out of the office, she had the chance to catch up without constant interruptions from the instant chat function on her system.

"I heard you were up here," Anastasia purred from the doorway.

Sabra looked up and had to blink to make sure she hadn't conjured the sex kitten from her imagination.

No such luck.

Anastasia was dressed in some designer snow suit that she'd made sure fit her waist, but that meant she had to keep the jacket open at her chest because her enhanced breasts didn't fit into the top.

"I work here," Sabra replied smoothly.

Anastasia smirked at her. "I know you *work* here." She looked around the office with disgust. "Just don't get too comfy. My daddy is going to make sure Tarak knows that keeping me happy means daddy's wallet is open." She flashed Sabra a bright smile of victory. "You'll be gone by tomorrow."

"We'll see."

Anastasia's smile faded, but her eyes filled with determination. "You're not worth millions of dollars. Do you really think Tarak runs all of this and doesn't know which wheels to grease? My daddy has connections all over the globe. He's the main buyer for most of the royal families outside the United States. You are so insignificant compared to us. Just wait until my daddy holds up ordering because of my injured feelings." She paused to smirk again. "That's when you'll get your pink slip."

"Well, we'll just see about that."

Sabra wished she felt as confident as she sounded, but she'd take the firm tone she replied in anyway. It was enough to sour Anastasia's expression. She hissed before turning around and disappearing.

That was a relief because Sabra was suddenly shaking.

Celeste's words rose from her memory like an alarm.

"Men with money always look out for one another. We are pets to their sort, nothing more."

She'd be a fool to overlook the merit locked up in reality. Tarak might care about her, but that wasn't love, and it wasn't likely to hold up against letting his business suffer.

He was Nektosha.

It was a fact that drew her to him and defined him.

Reality sucked.

———

Sabra packed up at five. The sun was down, but there was no snow blowing. She drove up to the cabin, trying her best not to dissolve into self-pity. She was dreading what hadn't even happened yet.

Yeah, but I'm not stupid either.

She kept her cell phones on the table, but they remained silent as she cooked dinner. The huge, ultra-plush cabin bored her without Tarak in it. The media center didn't beckon to her, and she ended up just staring at the view from the picture windows.

Her personal phone chirped at last. She jammed her thigh into the corner of the table as she raced around to grab the call before it went to her voice mail.

"Hey, Celeste."

"Sabra, you need to get to the airport."

The tone of her friend's voice was one she knew too well. It sent a chill of dread through her body that settled in her stomach. "Why?"

"Your father is going into surgery first thing in the morning."

"What?" Sabra yelled into the phone. "He swore he'd call me!"

"I thought he hadn't called you," Celeste confirmed. "He's so stubborn. He went to see a second specialist today who admitted him and told him if he went home, he'd better fill out his last will and testament because he'd be lucky to open his eyes in the morning. He's using the no cell phone rule at the hospital to avoid calling you."

"He promised me." But she couldn't be too surprised. It was her dad. In his world, he took care of her. "I'm getting to the airport, Celeste. Thanks."

She took a moment to send a text to Tarak. Her heart was racing as she confirmed a seat on an outbound flight, but when she ended the call, there was still no response from him.

Which was an answer in itself. The man took calls twenty-four hours a day. He'd seen the text.

Obviously it was working out for him.

So she'd have to get on with what she needed to do.

Tears stung her eyes as she left the cabin. At least there was no one to hide them from until she made it to the airport. The last thing she did was seal the keys to the truck in a prepaid envelope and drop them into a mailbox. It was a sad end, but the pain ripping through her heart promised her that at least for her, it was far from over.

She checked her phone at least a hundred times before switching it off for departure. But there was nothing.

Nothing, that was, except the crack in her heart.

Anastasia was waiting for Tarak when her father finally called it a night.

"Forget whatever it is you planned to say," he informed her.

Anastasia enacted a perfect shocked look, but he knew it was a sham. He held up a single finger, and she shut her mouth right on cue.

"You've made a grave error in setting your father on me. I'll tell you what I just told him. If he wants to walk away and spend his money somewhere else, do it. I'm not a gigolo and he should really teach you not to hire your dates."

Her face turned red. "You had no right!" she sputtered. "After I came all the way up to this shithole!"

"You don't get it, Anastasia. This is the cradle of Nektosha. It's where the next generation is forged. I can't be serious with anyone who doesn't understand that."

"Is that why you brought your little slut up here? Because she puts up with this frozen wasteland?" Anastasia snarled. "If she claims to like it, she's lying. No woman would like it here."

The door behind Anastasia opened, revealing her father. His face had darkened as he listened to his daughter.

"Anastasia Victoria, it's time for you to go to bed," he directed.

"But, *Daddy*."

He made a slashing motion with his hand. "It is done. Go to bed. Tomorrow, we'll discuss your future. It is time for you to grow up."

She clenched her fists but turned and hurried off, her spike heels clicking on the hallway floor.

Her father remained, looking pensive for a long moment.

"You have brass balls," he said at last. "Part of me wants to smash my knee into them, but the other part of me realizes my daughter used you as much as you used her—so no smashing. Anastasia must accept the risks of the games she plays. My assistant will have the order to you in a few days."

The door closed softly, granting Tarak some much-needed peace. He raked his fingers through his hair and grabbed his keys. The office was lit only by security lighting, but he didn't care. It was after two in the morning, and the darkness suited the moment.

The light he craved was at home.

The cabin came into view and he realized that it was Sabra who made it a home.

But the cabin was empty. He turned on all the lights, searching every last room for her. Hell, it even felt as if she were gone. Pain slashed through his heart, a pain he recalled feeling only once before.

Only this time it hurt a hundred times worse.

He yanked his cell phone out of his pocket and cussed when he saw the text message from her.

He cussed louder when he read it.

Only a client with the sort of money Anastasia's father had made him turn off his cell phone. The man wasn't ordering just for himself but for several other clients. It was something that would be changing just as soon as he caught up with Sabra.

His night assistant picked up on the first ring.

"Good evening, Mr—"

"Get my plane ready for takeoff. I need to go to Los Angeles."

"Yes, sir."

―⁓―

Hospitals were always cold.

After Alaska, Sabra wasn't sure why she thought the waiting room was chilly, but it was.

She paced and walked around the small waiting room. The clock on the wall moved at a snail's pace. What worried her most was the way a young priest walked by every so often and looked in to see if he might be needed.

She couldn't lose her dad and Tarak on the same day. Tarak was already doing enough damage.

Noon came and went, and so did the young priest again.

Her sanity was being stretched to its limits. She was sure she could hear the second hand on the clock moving. Another set of steps grated on her ears as someone approached the door of the waiting room. She turned around and walked the other way, not wanting to see the young priest again. She wasn't going to need his solace.

Nope.

She refused to allow the idea into her thoughts.

Which left her nothing to contemplate but Tarak.

His face filled her thoughts—the way he grinned when she broke through his stern exterior and the way he looked when he was hungry for her. Every intense moment. It was all etched into her mind so deeply—she drew in a ragged breath as her emotions shredded in response. When she turned back around, all she saw was him.

"We both have issues with checking our phones," he said

"I didn't realize you were… real."

It sounded lame. Really, really lame, but she was so happy to see him, all she could do was smile.

"You were thinking about me?" he asked quietly.

She nodded and stopped as she bit her lower lip.

His eyes suddenly brightened. "You should turn your phone on, Sabra. I've been trying to reach you for hours."

"Wait a minute." She looked up at the clock. "How did you get here so fast?"

"I keep a private jet at the test site." He ran a hand through his hair. "I only got you a commercial airline ticket so that you wouldn't argue with me about there being a paper trail at the office. With a private jet, I don't have to make a connection in British Columbia and lose three hours. I just had to wait for LAX to approve my landing."

"Oh… that's right." He was standing so close it was easy to lean toward him. "Why… why are you here?"

"Why?" he demanded, his expression turning incredulous before she saw anger flashing through his eyes. "Because I'm a fucking fool not to have told you I love you."

He pulled her against him, crushing her in an embrace that betrayed just how much emotion he had buried inside him.

"I swear, Sabra, I will check my messages from now on. I'm just used to Nektosha being the number one thing in my life." He kissed her temple and her cheek and her forehead before giving her space. "Just forgive me this time for not being there for you. I promise it will not happen again. You are the number one thing in my life. I can't live without you."

Her brain had stopped working. Shock held her in its grasp as he spoke every word she'd made up logical reasons for him never to say.

Even if it didn't make sense to her head, her heart responded in a flash. Tears eased from her eyes, and he wiped them aside with his thumbs.

"Don't cry, Sabra."

"I can't help it; you just made me the happiest woman alive."

She reached for him, gripping his wide shoulders and pulling him to her with hands that shook. He folded her back into his embrace, shielding her from everything and completing her.

"I never thought you'd—What about Anastasia?"

He set her back and reached down to pull a few tissues out of a box sitting on a small table. She wiped her eyes with them before realizing his expression had hardened.

"I told you not to worry about her," he growled softly. "That's why you didn't come over to the test track before leaving?"

"It's not like her reasoning wasn't... logical." The very fact that he was standing there made her feel foolish.

"I love you. Logic doesn't factor in." He reached into her purse and pulled her cell phone out and turned it on. "I started sending messages the moment I left her father and turned my cell phone on."

Sabra grabbed the phone and turned it off. "We're in a hospital, Tarak. No cell phones."

He glared at her for a moment before he raised his hands in surrender. "I hope you'll be patient with me, Sabra. I'm a little used to being in charge of everything. You'll have to train me on the more personal points of being a husband."

Her mouth went dry. "Husband?"

He tilted his head to one side before reaching out to cup the sides of her face. "I love you. Say you'll marry me, or am I sucking at the asking part again?"

"I love you, just the way you are."

He sealed her lips beneath his, giving her what had to be the very first sweet kiss they'd ever shared.

It was totally frickin' awesome.

—⁓—

"I tell you, this is no shit…"

Two weeks later, her father was sitting up and back to telling navy stories. Tarak was sitting by her father's bedside, hanging on every word. Her dad launched into a maritime tale that had his eyes sparkling by the time he finished it. He slapped the bed when he was done and looked at Tarak.

"Enough of this. You're doing a good job of listening to an old man, but I want to see a ring on my daughter's finger. Go jewelry shopping."

"You just want to flirt with the nurses," Sabra accused.

Her father waggled his gray eyebrows. "Have you seen that blond?" He whistled low and made a curvy hourglass with his hands. He winked at Tarak. "Get me a business card from the jeweler. I might need it."

"Dad, I think—"

"Off with you, my girl, you're the princess of sunshine, not stale hospital rooms. I'm going to take a nap and dream of fishing up there in Alaska on my son-in-law's property."

Tarak held out a hand for her and she took it, still absorbing the fact that he was hers.

"I don't need to go ring shopping."

"Yes you do," he assured her. "You need to have a huge diamond on your hand before I take you over to Angelino's. Nartan has been bugging me to drop by, but there is no way I'm letting him near you without a little repellant flashing on your hand. He's an incurable romantic. He said to invite your friend Celeste to even out the party."

"Um… that's not going to happen."

They'd reached the parking garage and Tarak opened the Aston Martin door for her. "Why not?"

"Celeste is a bit of a recluse when it comes to men who want to get to know her better. Her ex was an asshole who abused her. He's in jail at the moment."

Tarak considered her for a moment.

"That will make our wedding interesting," he decided, "because Nartan sounded more than mildly interested in her. Believe me, Nartan doesn't back off any better than I do."

Tarak shut the door, giving her a chance to groan. Celeste was going to be her maid of honor and Nartan would be the best man. They'd already decided on an intimate wedding to be held on the Nektosha test facility.

Which would give Celeste no place to hide from Nartan.

"Maybe we should get married here in California," Sabra suggested.

Tarak settled into the driver's seat. He turned and pegged her with a hard look. "Nartan won't get out of line."

"He's a lot like you," she accused softly. "And you get out of line all the time."

Something flickered in his eyes that sent a touch of heat across her cheeks. His attention shifted to the blush, and his expression softened.

"Relax, Sabra. It's worked out just fine for us. Maybe you should let fate have a shot at your friend."

"Celeste is my best friend, my sister really. She's got some deep wounds."

"Sheltering her isn't being a good friend." Tarak turned the engine on. "Nartan taught me that. I went to see him before I took off for Alaska, and he told me flat out that I was hung up on you. That's true friendship."

"Celeste isn't hung up on Nartan."

Tarak pulled out of the parking space. "Then there shouldn't be any problem with her being around him for a week."

"I guess."

"Aren't you the one who insisted I stop sharing my life with a ghost from my past?" He cut her a sidelong look.

"Yeah, I did."

Tarak nodded and wheeled the Aston Matron into traffic. "It was good advice. Use it on your friend."

He was right, but she still felt a shiver working along her spine. "Celeste's ghosts are more of the demon sort."

"In that case, I'm sure it's a good idea for the pair of them to be tossed together. Fears need to be faced." His lips curved into a satisfied smile. "You taught me that."

Her lips curved as a bubble of happiness burst inside her. It was an insane sort of delight and made her want to giggle. Somehow, she'd never realized how much happiness might be hers if she found the man she could love. It was amazing, and she wanted that for Celeste too.

"Alaska wedding it is."

About the Author

Dawn Ryder is the erotic romance pen name of a bestselling author of historical romances. She has been publishing her stories for over eight years to a growing and appreciative audience. She is commercially published in mass market and trade paper, and digi-first published with trade paper releases. She is hugely committed to her career as an author, as well as to other authors and to her readership. She resides in Southern California.

Against the Ropes

Sarah Castille

He scared me. He thrilled me. And after one touch, all I could think about was getting more...

Makayla never thought she'd set foot in an elite mixed martial arts club. But if anyone needs a medic on hand, it's these guys. Then again, at her first sight of the club's owner, she's the one feeling breathless.

The man they call Torment is all sleek muscle and restrained power. Whether it's in the ring or in the bedroom, he knows exactly when a soft touch is required and when to launch a full-on assault. He always knows just how far he can push. And he's about to tempt Makayla in ways she never imagined...

Praise for *Against the Ropes*:

"Smart, sharp, sizzling, and deliciously sexy."
—Alison Kent, bestselling author of *Unbreakable*

For more Sarah Castille books, visit:

www.sourcebooks.com

In Your Corner

Sarah Castille

A high-powered lawyer, Amanda never had any problem getting what she wanted. Until Jake. She was a no-strings-attached kind of girl. He wanted more. Two years after their breakup, she still hasn't found anyone nearly as thrilling in bed. And then he shows up in her boardroom…

Jake is used to fighting his battles in a mixed martial arts ring, not in court. He needs Amanda's expertise. And whether she knows it or not, she needs him to help her find true happiness.

For more Sarah Castille books, visit:

www.sourcebooks.com

Sinners on Tour

Hot Ticket

by Olivia Cunning

On stage, on tour, in bed, they'll rock your world...

A man as talented as Sinners bass guitarist Jace Seymour needs a woman who can beat out his self-doubt. A woman as strong as Mistress V needs a man she can't always overpower. And in each other's tight embrace, an escape from harsh reality is always a welcome diversion...

"The heat and hunger between the two leads creates a palpable tension that will keep readers turning pages with reckless abandon and begging for more from this sizzling series." —RT Book Reviews

"Cunning develops her characters into real people who engage in a compelling and satisfying erotic romance. Their relationship builds amid a dramatic series of unexpected events." —Publishers Weekly

"Sizzling hot, tragically emotional, and totally rockin'. Only one more band member to go and I can hardly wait." —Fresh Fiction

"I said it for the first book and I'll say it again, these yummy guys are so hot that you'll want to rip your clothes off and join them. I hope this tour never ends." —Night Owl Reviews, *Top Pick*

"As Jace's story is told in Hot Ticket, *the reader is provided with the heart-wrenching and powerful backstory that formed the Jace we saw in the first two books of this series."* —The Romance Reviews, *Top Pick*

For more Olivia Cunning, visit:

www.sourcebooks.com

Wicked Beat

Sinners on Tour

Olivia Cunning

New York Times and *USA Today* bestselling author

How far out are your fantasies?

When Rebeka Blake becomes the Sinners' new soundboard operator, she has no idea that red-hot drummer Eric Sticks is the only man who can give her everything her dirty mind desires...

Praise for *Double Time*:

"Olivia Cunning delivers the perfect blend of steamy sex, heartwarming romance, and a wicked sense of humor." —*Nocturne Romance Reads*

"Snappy dialogue, dizzying romance, scorching hot sex, and realistic observations about life on tour make this a winner." —*Publishers Weekly*

"It just doesn't get any hotter or any better. On- and offstage." —*Open Book Society*

"Smoking hot sex and romance that pulls at your heartstrings." —*Romance Reviews*

For more Olivia Cunning books, visit:

www.sourcebooks.com

Double Time

Sinners on Tour

Olivia Cunning

New York Times and *USA Today* bestselling author

He craves her music and passion

On the rebound from the tumult of his bisexual lifestyle, notoriously sexy rock guitarist Trey Mills falls for sizzling new female guitar sensation Regan Elliott and is swept into the hot, heady romance he never dreamed possible.

She can't get enough of his body

On the rebound from the tumult of his bisexual lifestyle, notoriously sexy rock guitarist Trey's band, The Sinners, Regan finds she craves Trey as much as she craves being in the spotlight.

They both need more…

When Regan's ex, Ethan Conner, enters the scene, Trey's secret desires come back to haunt him, and pleasure and passion are taken to a whole new level of dangerous desire.

For more Olivia Cunning books, visit:

www.sourcebooks.com

Rock Hard

Sinners on Tour

Olivia Cunning

New York Times and *USA Today* bestselling author

On stage, on tour, in bed, they'll rock your world...

Trapped together on the Sinners tour bus for the summer, Sed and Jessica will rediscover the millions of steamy reasons they never should have called it quits in the first place...

Praise for *Backstage Pass*:

"Olivia Cunning's erotic romance debut is phenomenal." —*Love Romance Passion*

"A sizzling mix of sex, love, and rock 'n' roll... The characters are irresistible. Can't wait for the second book!" —*DforDarla's Definite Reads*, 5 Stars

"These guys are so sensual, sexual, and yummy. This series...will give readers another wild ride..." —*Night Owl Romance*, 5 Stars, Reviewer Top Pick

For more Olivia Cunning books, visit:

www.sourcebooks.com

Backstage Pass

SINNERS ON TOUR

By Olivia Cunning

"Olivia Cunning's erotic romance
debut is phenomenal."
—Love Romance Passion

• •

For him, life is all music and no play...
When Brian Sinclair, lead songwriter and guitarist of the
hottest metal band on the scene, loses his creative spark, it
will take nights of downright sinful passion to release his
pent-up genius...

She's the one to call the tune...
When sexy psychologist Myrna Evans goes on tour with the
Sinners, every boy in the band tries to woo her into his bed.
But Brian is the only one she wants to get her hands on...

Then the two lovers' wildly shocking behavior sparks the whole
band to new heights of glory... and sin...

• •

"These guys are so sensual, sexual, and yummy.
[T]his series... will give readers another wild ride,
and I can't wait!"
—Night Owl Reviews
5/5 Stars
Reviewer Top Pick

For more Olivia Cunning, visit:

www.sourcebooks.com

Where There's Smoke

by Karen Kelley

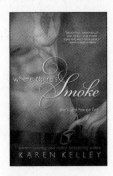

The Devil went down to Texas…

Sexy wannabe demon Destiny Carter has pissed off the people downstairs and has been kicked out of Hell. Now she's in Ft. Worth, Texas, with one week to corrupt a soul. Or else.

Lookin' for just One Soul to steal…

When smokin' hot Destiny strolls into The Stompin' Ground bar in a slinky red dress, she has a feeling her assignment might not be so bad. The cowboy at the bar looks pretty darn delicious and oh-so-corruptible.

But Chance Bellew is no ordinary cowboy, and Destiny gets way more than she bargained for when she rubs up against that sexy dark angel perched on a barstool like sin just waiting to happen…

"Kelley burns up the pages… This book is witty, sexy, and a lot of fun. Readers won't be able to wait to read the next installment!"
—RT Book Reviews, *4 stars*

"Bestseller Kelley (the Princes of Symtaria series) launches a sultry paranormal series with this smoky, sweet, and surprisingly touching tale."
—Publishers Weekly

For more Karen Kelley, visit:

www.sourcebooks.com

What a Goddess Wants

Forgotten Goddesses

by Stephanie Julian

—⁓—

In his arms, her magic powers are on the rise...

Tessa, Etruscan Goddess of the Dawn, is desperately fighting off a malicious god, but her powers are weakening. She needs a hero and fast, because only sexual energy can give her strength. So she seeks out Caligo, whose sexual prowess is legendary...

And she's the only one who can bring him into the light...

Caligo is a fabled Cimmerian warrior determined to stay away from spoiled goddesses who trample hearts after they've had their fun. But there's something irresistibly hot and inviting about Tessa, and he knows he's her only chance to escape the encroaching darkness...

—⁓—

Praise for Stephanie Julian:

"Sparkles with fantasy...and smoldering erotic scenes... unpredictable and fascinating." —*RT Book Reviews*

"Full of explosive passion...Ms. Julian gives readers what they want and so much more." —*Fallen Angel Reviews*

For more Stephanie Julian, visit:

www.sourcebooks.com

How to Worship a Goddess

Forgotten Goddesses

by Stephanie Julian

—ᔕᔕᔕ—

He's exactly what she's always wanted,
and she unleashes him like a force of nature...

Lucy was once the beloved Goddess of the Moon, and she could have any man she wanted. But these days, the goddesses of the Etruscan pantheon are all but forgotten. The only rituals she enjoys now are the local hockey games, where one ferociously handsome player still inflames her divine blood...

Brandon Stevenson is one hundred percent focused on the game, until he looks up and sees a celestial beauty sitting in the third row. A man could surely fall hard for a distraction like that...

—ᔕᔕᔕ—

Praise for Stephanie Julian:

"I'm hooked...wonderful romance with lots of interludes,
I anxiously await more." —*Night Owl Romance*

"Brutally vivid characters and flaming hot passion that
just leaps off the pages." —*Fallen Angel Reviews*

For more Stephanie Julian, visit:

www.sourcebooks.com

Goddess in the Middle

Forgotten Goddesses

by Stephanie Julian

—∿∿—

Together, they create the most powerful magic of all...

Romulus and Remus are sexy werewolf cousins with an unbreakable bond. When they meet beautiful goddess Amity and save her from an encroaching demon, they discover that the three of them together are way more powerful than any of them could ever have imagined. And they're going to need that power to overcome the forces that are determined to steal Amity's magic and destroy the two men. As different as night and day, and each an amazing man in his own right, Rom and Remy make all of Amity's deepest fantasies come true...

—∿∿—

Praise for the Forgotten Goddesses series:

"Oozing with sex and passion...it will knock your socks off!" —*The Romance Reviews*

"A thrilling and unique spin on the gods and goddesses of old...totally satisfying." —*Long and Short Reviews*

For more Stephanie Julian, visit:

www.sourcebooks.com

Awakening

by Elene Sallinger

He will open her eyes to the ultimate pleasure…

The minute Claire walked into his shop, she aroused every protective instinct Evan ever had. She looked so fragile, so lost. He ached to be the one to show her a world she'd never dreamed of, to awaken within her the passion she was so ripe to share. It only takes one touch for him to see how open and responsive she is to his dominant side. But the true test will be whether he can let go at last and finally open his heart…

Festival of Romance Award Winner

What readers are saying:

"If *Fifty Shades of Grey* intrigued you, *Awakening* will take you to a whole new level of desire, submission, and unforgettable romance."
—Judge, Festival of Romance contest

"One of the absolute best BDSM novels I have read. (And I've read quite a few.) This one is absolutely amazing!" —Autumn Jean

"Finally! A well-told story that shows the characters' vulnerabilities and how they learned to trust and love again." —A. Hirsch

"Exquisitely beautiful, touchingly heart-wrenching, and hedonistic enough to keep your body on fire."
—*Coffee Time Romance*, starred review

For more Xcite Books, visit:

www.sourcebooks.com

Restless Spirit

Sommer Marsden

Three men want her. Only one can truly claim her.

When Tuesday Cane inherits a cozy lake house, she's not expecting to find love as part of her legacy. But how can she choose between Aiden, the loyal and über-sexy handyman she's known for years; the charming and wealthy Reed Green, a former TV star; and the mysterious Shepherd Moore, an ex cage fighter.

The only way to know for sure is to try them all... Surrounded by so many interesting men and erotic temptations, Tuesday has no intention of committing. But deep down she longs for that special, soul-deep connection. Only, which man can entice this restless spirit into finally settling down?

What readers are saying:

"An intense emotional and sexual journey
that is quite compelling." —Kathy

"One of the best adult/erotica books I have ever read.
The characters are real and believable, and the sex
scenes are absolutely scorching hot." —Rebecca

"Themes of domination and submission are fantastically well
varied throughout the story... Realistic and relatable characters
with steamy encounters at every turn." —Michelle

For more Xcite Books, visit:

www.sourcebooks.com